THE SMALL HOURS

BOB PASTORELLA

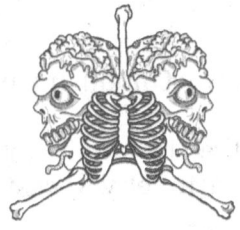

Ghoulish Books
San Antonio, Texas
1
The Smal Hours
Copyright © 2025 Bob Pastorella

First Edition

All Rights Reserved

ISBN: 978-1-963801-11-8

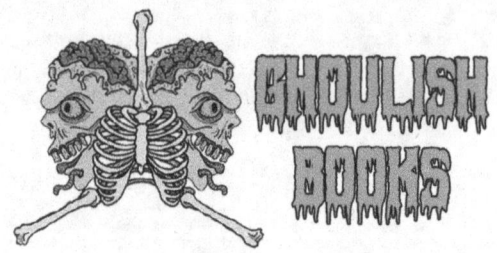

www.Ghoulish.rip

Edited by Mindy Rose
Cover art: Betty Rocksteady

Also by Bob Pastorella

Mojo Rising

They're Watching
(with Michael David Wilson)

PART ONE:

THE NIGHTCOMERS

CHAPTER ONE

JAY WAS SURE he saw LuCyndi's t-shirt in Mr. Fields' backyard shed.

What's she wearing now? That made sense because she couldn't be dead, right? Your friends don't get killed by serial killers, that's something that happened to other people. But there was a funeral, not even two weeks ago. Closed casket, which never really seals the deal. What's the word . . . closure? The word felt too final, a word Jay refused to let his mind wrap around.

It didn't make sense. Why would her shirt be in Mr. Fields' shed?

And it was a glimpse, a fleeting image at the corner of his eye, but enough for Jay to make the connection. It was the small hole in the sleeve. A black Lacuna Coil shirt faded grey from repeated washing, a ragged hole on the sleeve from a cigarette burn. He'd know that shirt anywhere because it was his cigarette that had caused the burn, and it was now tossed aside like LuCyndi's life, sitting on the workbench in a shed of a strange man Jay already had bad feelings about.

Mr. Fields, with his weird accent.

Mr. Fields, always going out of town.

Mr. Fields, inviting people to his house. Jay couldn't watch his neighbor's house all the time, but he watched enough to know more people entered than left.

Mr. Fields was Russian mafia.

It made sense. He was a hitman, probably got off on

the killing. Fields probably wasn't even his real name. A Russian mafia serial killer. The truth couldn't have been simpler.

But first, Jay needed evidence.

You can't go around accusing people with weird accents and strange habits of being in the Russian mafia. Especially a man with a Blue Lives Matter sticker in the center of his rear windshield. Fields drove an older model Audi, no dents or scratches, the only blemish was the sticker placed perfectly in line of sight to be noticed. Fields probably donated money to the sheriff's department.

Currently between jobs and semesters, Jay spent his weekdays landscaping the neighborhood. Except for Mrs. Teller's house. She paid more for a professional lawn care service. She never liked Jay much anyway, and she *really* didn't like Willi. Mrs. Teller was a racist old bitch who probably ate TV dinners and drank wine until she passed out every night. Most people paid Jay thirty to forty dollars cash to cut and trim. Mr. Fields always paid more, a crisp fifty-dollar bill once a week. He folded the bill lengthwise like he was tipping a stripper and kept it in the front inside pocket of his jacket. Fields wore a suit and tie every single day. Nice cufflinks to attract roaming eyes away from the tattoos on the back of his hands and fingers—though maybe Fields thought he was enhancing the tattoos.

Another sign pointing to the Russian mob.

It was December, two weeks before Christmas, and the grass was dying or already dead. Most of the people in the neighborhood had been turning Jay away for a couple of weeks. Mr. Fields was the only one who wanted his grass cut before Christmas.

Jay cut the grass, then used the weed wacker to trim around the edges where the row of shrubs stood out from Fields' front porch. Then he trimmed the backyard along the fence and around the patio. His trimmer line broke as he neared the shed. While untangling the line inside the trimmer head, Jay realized there wasn't enough left to finish the job, so he went into the shed to refill.

That was when he saw LuCyndi's shirt.

The front of the shed was where Fields kept his tools, mostly old brooms and rakes, a shovel that had seen better days, and a workbench littered with rusted pliers and screwdrivers, snips of wire and screws on the worn counter. An old vise without a crank handle sat at the end, its jaws rusted shut. Among the clippings of wire and screws, a faded black t-shirt was rolled into a loose ball, the right sleeve hanging off the edge of the bench with Jay's cigarette burn prominently on display. Beyond the workbench was a large, heavy canvas tarp, hung over a thick cord that separated the front of the shed from the rear. The tarp was pushed aside like a curtain, and for the first time Jay could see what lay at the rear of the shed. The walls were bare, and a cardboard box filled with cans of spray paint sat in front of a door with several locks on it. The door looked like it could withstand a tornado. Probably made of solid steel.

What was Fields hiding behind that door?

Drugs?

Money?

Jay imagined garbage bags bulging with cash, or shrink-wrapped cardboard boxes packed with strapped bills. That's how they did it, or at least how they did it according to the gospel of *Ozark*. It was easy to picture Fields laundering money. Quiet little Grigsby, Texas. Local 5-O on the take. Yearly contributions to the election fund of whoever was buying.

Happens every single day.

A hand shot over Jay's shoulder and gripped the side of the tarp, pulling it shut. Jay jumped, surprised to find Fields standing behind him.

Fields held the roll of trimmer line in his hand. "Looking for this?"

"Ah, yeah. Almost done."

"I'm going out of town for the holiday, but I'll be hosting a small party after Christmas. The grass . . . it's dead." He pointed to the driveway. "See how the weeds travel on the drive?"

Jay nodded.

"Make them go away."

"You want me to spray some weedkiller?"

Fields shook his head. "Then I wouldn't need your services so often. I know things are rough for you . . . for everyone. You should be in school, at a real job, with insurance and good pay. Don't shoot your own foot. The winter will be mild and the grass will return, as all dead things do in one way or another. Am I right?"

"Right."

"Then it's settled." Fields handed him the trimmer line. "When you finish, I have a treat for you."

A treat?

Jay nodded and went back to work.

After he was done, Jay headed to the back yard to put up the trimmer. Mr. Fields was sitting on one of the reclining loungers on the patio, drinking a beer. He had taken off his jacket, loosened his tie, and rolled up his sleeves.

Jay shut the door to the shed, snapped the padlock, and wiped his hands on his pants. He'd worked up a sweat despite the nip in the air. He was nervous and wanted to get the hell out of there.

Fields motioned for Jay to join him on the patio. "Are you twenty-one yet?"

"March," Jay said, trying to keep the conversation to a minimum.

"Ah, so close. Well, today, since it is nearly Christmas, we'll say it's your birthday." He handed Jay a bottle from the table next to the lounger. "Merry Christmas and happy birthday."

Jay accepted the bottle. It wasn't like he could turn the man down. He had to act like it was all business as usual.

The beer was Dos Equis, brown label. Not as crisp as the green, but still mighty fine after a day of yard work. "Thank you." He looked around as though his mom was watching, then took a sip.

"It's good, huh?"

"Yes." Was this the treat Fields had mentioned? Seeing him sitting there, with tattoos on his forearms and peeking out from under his shirt collar, Jay wondered exactly what other treats Fields had in mind. He looked like Jack Nicholson from that bloody backroom scene in *The Departed*.

"Do you like seafood?" Fields asked.

Jay nodded. "It'll be crawfish season soon."

Fields smiled. "Oh yes. I'll be going to Mae's this season for sure. So good." Fields took a sip of beer. "Do you like oysters?"

"Hmmm, I've had them fried."

"On the half-shell?"

Jay shook his head, sipped his beer. "Can't say that I have."

"Come inside, I have a treat for you."

Jay finished off his beer, maybe a little too quickly, then tried to hand the empty bottle back to Fields. "I really should head on out, got some things to take—"

Fields took the bottle and handed Jay another, cutting him off. "C'mon now, it's Christmas break. An appetizer, certainly nothing that would spoil your dinner."

Jay didn't see how he had much of a choice. Fields was about as tall as Jay but probably fifty to sixty pounds heavier. Not fat, but solid. Willi always called Jay scrawny, which he usually hated to hear, but now he had to admit it fit him like a glove. No way he could take Fields on. Not without a weapon.

Jay was scared.

Of what? He didn't know.

That's Luce's shirt in his shed. You know it is.

But what if it wasn't? What if he was seeing things?

Maybe it was just a balled-up old rag that looked like her shirt. And even if it was her shirt, what about it? The police wouldn't be able to do anything without probable cause. He needed something else, something tangible.

Something damning.

Maybe there was something inside the house, something else that could link Fields to LuCyndi.

Sure, justify it however you need to.

And now he was thinking of having to 'take Fields on'? What the hell was that all about?

Jay followed Fields inside, sipping his beer and acting like he didn't have a care in the world. Fields closed the back door behind him, then slid in front of Jay. The kitchen had one of those island things, with a double sink and a range in the center, a large granite countertop for the workspace. Cabinets ran along the walls. There were several folded towels on the countertop, with one large towel covering something lumpy. Fields walked over to the refrigerator and started grabbing things from the inside of the door. He sat bottles of cocktail sauce and horseradish on the counter next to the Tabasco and Frank's Hot Sauce. "I don't like any hot sauce other than Frank's, but if you don't like it, I have the other brands."

"Frank's is good."

"The best." Fields lifted the large towel, revealing a platter of oysters on ice. There were probably two dozen of them. Fields picked one up. "Curious animals here. They have a secret I'll tell you about after you try one." He placed the oyster on a towel and grabbed a knife from the block on the counter. The knife's handle was thick and round while the blade was short. Both edges looked razor-sharp.

Was Fields about to slit his throat? Is that what all the towels were for?

Fields placed the tip of the blade between the halves of the oyster and gently twisted his wrist, popping it open. He then slid the blade in, passing it quickly side-to-side. The oyster shell split, revealing the soft meat inside. A quick cut of the blade underneath the meat released it from the shell. Fields quickly grabbed another oyster and shucked it the same way. He passed Jay one of the half-shells.

"Pour a little Frank's on it. Or . . . cocktail sauce, horseradish if you really want to spice it up."

Jay dabbled a couple of drops of Frank's on the oyster. Fields applied a large dollop of the same on his.

"Tip the shell into your mouth. Don't think about it, just swallow."

Anything to get the hell out of Fields' house. Jay tipped the shell into his mouth, feeling the cold meat, almost liquid in consistency, hit his tongue. It was strange drinking something raw, the bright taste of iron coating his mouth. Then the Frank's sauce hit, and he swallowed.

The flavor, initially *squishy*, was damn good.

"Well?"

Jay smiled. "That was great."

"Aha, see . . . I knew you'd like them. Good treat then?"

Jay nodded. "Yes sir."

"Another?"

Jay watched Fields open a couple more oysters and tried it again, this time with a little dab of cocktail sauce. Fields inspected a couple of the oysters, then placed them back on the ice. He finally settled on one and showed it to Jay. "See how the shell is slightly open?"

Jay nodded.

Fields tapped the top of the shell with the knife handle. The shell quickly shut.

"Does that mean it's a bad one?" Jay asked.

"No. If there is a strong odor, like sulfur, then you cannot eat it."

"You throw them away then?"

"Usually. Sometimes you can cook them with batter, but I'd rather not take the chance. See, when they have that odor, that means they are dead."

Jay smiled. "Well, these are all dead."

Fields started laughing. "If these do not have the odor,

then they are not dead. That can only mean that they are alive. That is the secret of the oyster. They are best when alive. Of course, they die quickly once you eat them, but to eat something alive, to hold that power over them, it's invigorating."

Jay thought he was going to throw up. "You're kidding, right?"

"That is something I never do. I never kid about anything. The truth is strange, is it not?"

Jay's phone rang in his pocket, the sudden shrill nearly causing him to drop his beer. "Excuse me a sec?" He couldn't remember a time he was so glad to see his mother's name pop up on his caller ID. "Hey?" he said into the phone. "Oh, really. I didn't think she was going to make it in so soon. Sure. Okay . . . on my way." He hung up and looked at Fields. "My girlfriend is back sooner than I expected."

Mr. Fields raised his eyebrows. "The beautiful negro girl?"

Jay winced. "Well, she's mixed race, but she prefers black."

"But of course, I meant no disrespect. Her name is Willi?"

How did Fields know that? "She's waiting over at my house, and Mom forgot the breadsticks, so . . . "

"Of course." Fields grabbed another oyster and started working on the shell. "Best not to keep such a pretty girl waiting."

"Same time next week?"

"No. The week after that would be fine. Maybe you could help me with the leaves in the gutters. I'll pay you extra for the work. We'll work on them together?"

Jay nodded. He was so ready to get out of Fields' house. "See you then."

"See you soon, and Merry Christmas."

CHAPTER TWO

WILLI WAS HELPING Jay's mom in the kitchen when he got home. She had her massive mane pulled back from her face, glasses perched at the end of her nose, and one of Jay's old t-shirts thrown on. Willi could wear a garbage bag and make it look great. Mom was at the stove, stirring a large pot of sauce; Willi was working on the salad.

"Hey," Jay said, slamming the front door shut for effect.

Willi set the knife down and abandoned the tomato she was dicing. She rushed up to Jay and hugged him tightly, giving him a little peck at the corner of his mouth. They had a rule: no P.D.A. around Mom. Holding hands and little kisses were okay, nothing too awkward. "Hey yourself," Willi said.

"I didn't expect you back so soon."

"Well, this was supposed to be a surprise. I told her I didn't mind picking up the breadsticks, but she wouldn't let me go once I got here."

"Jay's a grown man, he can pick that stuff up and let us girls catch up, right?" Jay's mom said. As far as moms went, Jay's was pretty cool. She was a little older than most of his friends' mothers, but could hang with the best of them. Plus, she tried so hard to be a mother to Willi without overstepping any boundaries. Willi had been raised by her older sister since she was five. Her mother was dead, and her father was busy as hell with his job, though the last couple of years he'd been in Willi's life a little more, which was nice. Mr. Murray was not a bad father, it was mostly that he wasn't there for Willi because of circumstances, having a career with a lot of travel, long nights at the office when he was in town, those sorts of things. Jay didn't really understand, exactly, what the guy did for a living, if he was being honest. Seemed like a lot of people depended on him, but other than that, Jay didn't have a clue. Willi's sister had done a fine job raising her, though. Willi was the most driven, resourceful person Jay knew, and that she put up with his utter lack of initiative amazed him to no end.

"Sure, Mom, keep me from the girl of my dreams."

"The woman of your dreams," Willi corrected, with a sly smile on her face.

Jay pulled Willi closer. "We need to talk. Important."

"Okay, we will." Willi's eyes widened. "Hey . . . hey, you're shivering."

Jay tried to keep his composure. "It's about LuCyndi."

Willi's lips narrowed, smile evaporating. "What?"

"Not in front of Mom."

Jay's mom refused to let him help with the cooking, insisting he take a shower and get rid of the odor of a thousand goats that had followed him in. When he returned, clean and dressed in fresh clothes, Jay's mom was talking about how nice it would be if it snowed for Christmas.

"We go through this every year. It's not going to snow," Jay said.

"You never know," she said, in a hopeful sing-song voice.

"Two years ago we spent Christmas at Uncle Steve's beach cabin. In shorts."

"I remember that," Willi said.

"You probably remember it more from Uncle Steve getting drunk and going full-throttle asshole-mode at the dinner table."

"*Jay* . . . language."

"Sorry, Mom, but it's true."

Willi nodded. "It was pretty bad."

Jay's mom patted Willi on the shoulder. "Uncle Steve is not invited. He can go to Hell."

"Good," Jay said. "But it's not going to snow. Not now, not anytime soon. Forecast says it's going to be another typical Christmas. Rainy and cold, but no snow."

They ate dinner at the table, Jay's mom at the head. "Did you tell Jay the good news?"

Willi spun a meatball in the angel hair. "Not yet." She smiled at Jay. "I got a job."

Jay's eyes narrowed. "In College Station?"

Willi laughed. "Here, silly. I'm a reporter for the *Grigsby Gazette*. It's part-time, but it's a start."

"I thought the *Gazette* closed down."

Willi twirled another meatball. "Three issues a week plus Sundays. Print's not dead, yet."

"They should go digital. That's how all the major papers do it now."

Willi nodded. "I know this is a dead-end, but it'll look good on my resume, and the extra money won't hurt."

Jay smiled. "Either way, my girl's a damn reporter now. You're going to blow the lid off all the bullshit going on around here."

Jay's mom shot him a look of disapproval of his choice of wording, but smiled anyway.

"Whoa. I'm not covering crime, although I'd *love* to get that gig. I mean, that's my dream, especially with a focus on the victims."

"That's how Patton Oswalt's wife got started," Jay said.

"Her name was Michelle McNamara, rest her soul. She had a blog, her own thing going, far removed from Patton. Big difference. But yeah, in that vein, more personal. I'm going to write a piece about LuCyndi. Hopefully they'll run it, but no guarantees."

Jay's mom reached over and touched Willi's hand. "It's

so good to hear you're writing about her, I just hope you don't get . . . well, you know . . . "

"I want to find out who killed her."

Jay's mom squeezed Willi's hand. "I know, I know. That's the focus. Justice."

Willi nodded, and for a second looked like she was going to cry. She shut her eyes and Jay fought back the urge to run to her side and comfort her. Instead, he reached across the table and held her other hand. After a few seconds, she snapped her eyes open. "They'll find him," she said.

"The police? They haven't done shit. You'll find him. *We'll* find him," Jay said.

Jay's mom cleared her throat, doing her best to steer the conversation in a different direction. "Have you always liked to write?"

Willi shrugged. "Off and on. More on lately. Mostly personal stuff, some poetry."

"I'd love to read your poems."

Willi shook her head. "Um, no . . . they're not for public consumption."

"They're love poems about me," Jay said, reaching for a breadstick while dragging his sleeve through the sauce on his plate. Willi started laughing. "What?" Jay asked.

"You're going to have to change your shirt," she said, pointing at his sleeve.

Jay looked at his arm. "Dammit."

After they cleared the table, Jay clicked on the news. LuCyndi's story wasn't featured on any of the local news anymore. Buried and forgotten. He wondered what the police were doing about it. No doubt they were focused on the latest breaking news. Two elementary school kids missing, Carmen Garcia and Timothy Rice. Concerned parents were fixated on a strange lady seen around the playgrounds in town. A few other kids claimed to have seen her, said she told them weird things and smelled like garbage. The police had no leads but cautioned parents to not let their kids wander unsupervised, especially after dark, which was when the sightings had occurred. Now there was a curfew, and police warned about homeless people in the parks, usually looking for money or items they could steal for drugs.

There was real crime happening in Grigsby and the police were worried about homeless people scrounging for change?

Jay felt Willi's hands on his shoulders. She smelled of liquid detergent and garlic. "Girl, you need to wash your hands."

"I did." She sat next to him on the sofa. "What's going on?"

Jay kept his voice so his mom wouldn't hear him from the kitchen. "I think I saw LuCyndi's shirt in Mr. Fields' shed."

Willi took a deep breath. "Not this crap again. You can't keep going around thinking everyone in town is a Russian spy."

"Not a spy. The mob."

"Whatever."

"Big difference. No doubt there are Russian spies among us in the states. But the mob is here, in Grigsby. Anyway, it's that Lacuna Coil shirt." Despite a lack of physical evidence, there was a CCTV image of LuCyndi exiting a place of business in that exact shirt the day she went missing. The local news stations circulated that grainy image to help locate her.

"What makes you so sure it was her shirt?"

"The cigarette burn."

"Lots of shirts have cigarette burns."

"On the sleeve? The cigarette burn from my cigarette when she and Quinten went on their first date?"

"Last date."

"Doesn't matter. It's her shirt."

Jay remembered exactly how her shirt had gotten the cigarette burn. They'd been coming home from a night drinking at Barlow's Billiards. LuCyndi had just broken up with her long-time boyfriend Arty and had agreed to go out with Jay's asshole buddy Quinten. Jay knew the Quinten thing would never work, especially if Willi had anything to say about it. It wasn't that it couldn't work, with Quinten's chiseled good looks and LuCyndi's infectious green eyes. Both were extremely popular, especially in the athletic department. They looked good together. It was more like they were the ends of two repelling magnets, doomed to attract, but never making that ultimate connection. Eventually, one of those magnets would spin the other way, and that magnet was of course LuCyndi. She was bound to be with Arty, but Quinten was going to try his best anyway. This was the first time LuCyndi had been single since he'd started crushing on her since eighth grade, so it was now or never.

Willi reluctantly agreed to double up with them after she learned LuCyndi wanted to play some pool. "She's going to slaughter his arrogant ass," she flashed a crooked smile, "just you wait and see."

LuCyndi did indeed slaughter Quinten at the table. Unfortunately, it only made him try harder to gain her attention.

Claiming Jay was too drunk, Willi insisted on driving them home that night. Jay wasn't that drunk, but he was too tired to argue with Willi. He remembered lighting a cigarette, cracking the window to let the smoke out. LuCyndi immediately started bitching about the smoke from the backseat, and the music. LuCyndi was deaf in her left ear and wore a hearing aid that constantly needed fresh batteries.

"Turn it up," LuCyndi said.

Jay had it set to the classic rock station out of Houston. "They're playing a commercial."

"Turn it up anyway, I can't hear shit with all this smoke."

That made Quinten crack up. Jay looked at his buddy

in the backseat, trying to gauge his progress. Things were not working out too well for Quinten. He was sitting as far from LuCyndi as he could get, hands folded in his lap. Jay caught his eye and Quinten shrugged.

Oh well.

"Turn it up," LuCyndi said again. She was wearing a dirty old trucker hat backwards, hair in braids. Jay turned back around and was reaching for the volume to turn up the music when LuCyndi's arm shot across the console from the rear seat. Her arm hit the cigarette hanging from the corner of Jay's mouth. Embers flew from the end of the cigarette, littering the car and Willi's clothes. LuCyndi yelped and sat back down, rubbing her arm.

"You fucked up my shirt," she said, slurring her words. She was very drunk, and Jay knew she could be extremely unpredictable when she was drunk. Best not to piss her off any further.

They spent the rest of the ride in silence. It was the last time LuCyndi and Quinten went on an actual date, though they remained good friends, just as before.

"I remember that night," Willi said. She clasped her hands together and squeezed them tight, a sign she was beginning to lose her patience. "Okay, say this is LuCyndi's shirt. It doesn't mean Mr. Fields was involved."

"Of course it does. Look, you're the reporter . . . this could be your big break."

"Human interest stories. That's my job. The 'little old lady retiring from the library' stories"

"So. Doesn't mean you can't branch out. Don't you see, this could be the clue that could break the case open."

"Then we tell the police."

Jay shook his head. "No. Definitely not. One hundred percent not. If he's the mob, then that could be bad."

"That's what the police are for."

"What if they're involved?"

"Huh? Do you even hear yourself?"

"If he's mobbed up, and if we go to the police, they'll

probably question him. They'll get a search warrant and check out his property. The shed is huge, like there's this massive metal door with a bunch of locks on it in the back. What's he hiding in there? They'll get a search warrant for that, maybe. Fields is going to suspect someone ratted him out. He's going to think it's me because I'm the only person who's been in his shed."

"That you know of."

"Still, why risk it? If he did it, and he suspects it was me who ratted him out, that could put us all in danger. He'll come after us."

Willi rolled her eyes. "Good god, listen to yourself. You've got to lay off those tv series. All the *Narcos* and *Breaking Bad* shit has gone to your head."

"*Narcos* is about Pablo Escobar, and—"

"You know what I'm talking about." She continued to squeeze her hands together, her knuckles turning white.

Jay grabbed her hands and held them.

"This is crazy," Willi said.

"Don't you want to know who killed her?"

Willi took a deep breath. "Of course."

"This could be a lead."

"But what if it's not."

"But what if we know and didn't do anything and he kills another girl? Have the police done anything so far? No."

Jay could see Willi was close to getting pissed off. She unclasped her hands and took a few deep breaths. "What exactly is it you want to do?"

Jay smiled. "I want to break into his shed and get that shirt."

CHAPTER THREE

WILLI LOOKED AT Jay as though he had completely lost his mind. "Are you fucking crazy?"

"No. I want to get the evidence."

"What you're proposing is evidence tampering. Sneaking into someone's property and taking something from them, even if you think it's evidence of a crime, is illegal. Now you want to commit crimes, B&E and tampering with evidence. We need to tell the police."

"Listen, I got it all figured out."

"Oh please, do share the foolproof plan you just thought of that's doomed to fail."

"Listen. Okay, so we don't take the shirt. There's a chance he may have moved it."

"What makes you think that?"

"Because when I saw it, he was in the shed with me. He might have realized what I was looking at."

Willi narrowed her eyes. "You didn't know he was in there?"

"No, he snuck up behind me. Then he gave me a beer and we ate oysters."

"Oysters?"

"I couldn't just leave, then he'd have *really* suspected something was up."

"*Oysters?*"

"Yeah, on the half-shell. Did you know they're alive until you eat them?"

Willi looked like she was going to throw up. "What does that have to do with anything?"

"It was what he was talking about. Really creepy shit, about eating life, controlling it. He's a psychopath."

"Okay, you thought you saw LuCyndi's shirt and you noticed a door with a bunch of locks, then he snuck into the shed with you and you got drunk with him and ate oysters? Are you sure you didn't imagine this shirt?"

"I'm sure."

"Listen. Mr. Fields is weird, no doubt about it. He's not from around here, but he's made some good friends and does a lot of business here obviously."

"What's his business?"

Willi looked at her hands. "I don't know . . . banking?"

"He's in shipping. Exports, imports. And he makes a ton of money doing it. That's what drug dealers do."

"I thought he was in the Russian mob?"

"It's all tied together."

"So why did he kill LuCyndi? What's his motivation?"

Jay smiled. "Look at my girl, talking about motivation and shit. I don't know, but it's got to be tied together. I know I told you about all those people coming to his house. People show up, but they never leave."

"You mean you didn't see them leave."

"Whatever. Still, it's all tied together. Maybe he's a hitman, likes killing, and sometimes kills random people."

"A Russian mob serial killer? Oh, wait . . . a Russian mob drug dealing serial killer, who's in the import-export business. Makes sense."

"Why do you like Mr. Fields so much?"

Willi shook her head. "Maybe you should ask yourself why you *don't* like him? Maybe you don't like him because he's an immigrant."

Jay stared at Willi. "No. No no no . . . that's not it. You know better than that."

Willi wrapped her hands around Jay's face, cradling his cheeks like he was a small child having a tantrum. "Then what is it?"

Jay shrugged. "I don't know. Just a feeling, and it won't

go away. Listen. How about we get into his shed and take pictures of the shirt?"

"Still breaking and entering."

"But if we don't take anything, then it could have been anyone breaking and entering, right?"

Willi nodded. "Then what?"

"We take the pictures to the police."

"And they arrest you for breaking and entering."

"We send them to the police anonymously."

"How? Remember January 6th? The Capitol Siege? The police found nearly every single one of those motherfuckers from tracking their phones. What makes you think they won't know you sent the pictures?"

"We do it by mail."

Willi chewed on her nails, thinking. "When do you want to do this?"

"Tonight."

"Tonight?

"Fields is out of town for the next few days, he'll probably be back by Monday. The sooner we do it, the better."

Willi stood up and started pacing in front of the TV. Jay knew this look too well—she was about to start counting off points on her fingers. "Do you know if he has surveillance cameras around his property?" she asked.

"Not that I've ever seen. I've been spending a few hours there a week for the past five months, but I've only been inside once. There's a group of women who show up sometimes, probably with one of those cleaning companies. They've been there when he was out of town, and I remember them using a key to get into the house."

"Just because they used a key doesn't mean there's not a security system." Willi counted off to her next finger. "Are you sure this is a cleaning company? Do they ever do any work at night?"

"I guess they're a cleaning company. They're young

women, kinda pretty, and don't speak English, at least that I've heard."

"What the fuck does that have to do with anything?"

"Fields is Russian, so they probably speak Russian."

Willi stopped and put her hands on her hips. "Do you know Russian?"

"No, but I've heard it. I think I know what it sounds like."

She started pacing again. "Okay . . . we don't know about security, and there's a group of women who come by his house during the week who may or may not work for a cleaning crew, and who may or may not be Russian. Y'know, for someone who's spent a lot of time scoping this guy out, you don't seem to have any idea what's going on."

"Well, thanks. I can't just fucking ask the man if he's in the Russian mob."

Willi sat down on the sofa again. "Don't get mad, just think about what you're wanting to do."

She was right, he hadn't thought it through. "Help me make a plan."

"Who else have you seen over there?"

"No one." Jay thought about it for a second, then snapped his fingers. "Erick the Red."

"Who?"

Jay lowered his voice, hoping his mom was still out of earshot in the kitchen. "My weed dealer. I've seen him over there."

"You mean that old lanky stoner dude?"

"He's pretty cool actually. He's a guitarist, and his music collection is excellent."

Willi shook her head, then her eyes lit up. "Do you think he knows anything?"

Jay shrugged. "I think he's probably selling dope to Fields."

"Then this is good. He's compromised. He's a drug dealer, and if we need him, we can hold it over his head and make him talk to the police."

THE SMALL HOURS

Jay laughed. "The cops know Erick well. Dude never gets busted, probably sells to them."

"Betcha he doesn't sell to Detective Barnes." Barnes was well-known across Grigsby as *the* local hardass. He was a throwback to the days when cops were cops and criminals were afraid. His no-bullshit stance against drugs was legendary, especially after being involved with the Mojo Rising meth shit a few years back.

"The less we have to deal with Barnes, the better."

Willi smiled. "Oh, I agree . . . one hundred percent, but it's useful information. I wonder what this Erick guy knows about Fields."

"One way to find out."

Willi pursed her lips. She was thinking, Jay could see the wheels spinning in her eyes. "What's on your mind?" he asked.

"Okay, hear me out. If Fields is with the mob, like you say, then we need some backup."

Jay stared at her. His mouth went dry thinking how truly serious all this was. If Fields killed LuCyndi, how far would he go to protect himself? "This is dangerous. It's bad enough I've told you about any of this. In fact, the more I think about it, the less I want you involved. And I don't want anyone else involved either."

"Fuck that shit, I'm in this. LuCyndi was my best friend, no way I'm not bringing the fucker down if he's the one who did it."

He didn't like it. "Too dangerous."

"I know. And I'm not even sure I completely go along with everything you've told me so far. Still sounds farfetched. Like, this is some crazy ass shit. But . . . *but* . . . if there's even a remote possibility that you're right . . . that's a chance I'm willing to take. The police have nothing to go on, and if we can get them a lead, some real evidence . . . then . . . "

"And you want 'backup'?"

"Arty for sure. Definitely Quinten."

"But you hate him?"

"I do not. I . . . dislike him. He's a little rough around the edges. Okay, that's not fair to edges. He's a *lot* rough around the edges, but he's also a badass I'd want on my team if shit got serious."

Jay nodded. Arty would be down simply because he was LuCyndi's ex-boyfriend. They'd broken up on good terms and remained friends. Jay hadn't talked to Arty in a while, and the last time was enough to bring Jay to tears seeing how down Arty was after LuCyndi's death. It was so obvious he still had deep feelings for her. Jay heard Arty quit college and was barely leaving his apartment. He remembered hearing from Suzi Weatherford that Arty had been seen at the supermarket wearing his mask and gloves like he didn't want anyone to recognize him. "I need to see Arty anyway. And Quinten, well . . . you know he loves a good fight."

"And he has a gun."

"Guns."

Willi nodded. "We need a game plan. Has Fields left town yet?"

Jay shrugged.

"We need to make sure he's really gone before we do this. That's your job . . . just watch his house and make a note when he leaves. Shouldn't be too hard as you spy on him all the time as it is. Then, when we're positive Fields is out of town for the weekend, we get to work."

"We need to do it soon."

Willi stood up. "No shit. I want to make sure there aren't any security cameras set up first. We can do that the day after tomorrow. We'll make it look like we're finishing up the yard work so people don't get suspicious."

Jay's eyes grew wide. "The gutters! He wanted me to help him next week with the gutters. That'll be our excuse."

Willi smiled. "I'll help you with the gutters if you help me with something else."

Jay went to shake on it but stopped and pulled his

hand back. "Why do I feel I'm about to get the short end of the stick?"

"Okay . . . this is crazy, but I think everything might be related."

"Everything?"

"Luce's murder, the kids in the park. There's a connection there, it's just that no one can see it. When's the last time anything like this happened in Grigsby? Or anywhere? Remember the Atlanta child murders?"

Jay nodded. "They got the wrong guy. And the kids from Grigsby Park are just missing."

"As much as I hate to say this, you and I both know it's only a matter of time. God, I hope I'm wrong, but you know how these things turn out."

"Don't think that. Missing doesn't mean dead."

"Okay, okay. But with the Atlanta case, there's still a lot of evidence that suggests Wayne Williams did it all. And *this* is just like that case."

"What's happening here doesn't fit any profile—"

"But one person could have killed LuCyndi and taken those kids. Why is that so hard to believe with what's happening in Grigsby? That's why I brought up the Atlanta case. There are too many unanswered questions, yet everything fits if you look at the big picture."

Willi had a point. "What do we do?"

"Here's the deal . . . I have an interview with Frannie Garcia tomorrow, Carmen Garcia's mother. Someone else was going to cover it, but they're out of town and since it's more of a human-interest story, they let me have it. I have to do the job, get the information I'm there for." Willi took her phone from her pocket and showed Jay her voice recording app. "As long as she sees me turn this off, I think she'll open up, woman to woman. Still, we have to be careful, my boss said she was extremely reluctant to talk to anyone."

"And let me guess, you need a ride to her house?"

"To the church. She's the secretary for Saint Thomas Cathedral, and they're doing a fundraiser for the families."

Jay nodded. "I'm in."

"I'll say you're my photographer, so you're going to have to look nice."

Jay looked down at his clothes. "You mean like wear a suit? Fuck, I don't even have a camera."

"Nooo . . . but at least shave and wear a nice shirt. Tucked in. Bring your phone and take a picture of her for the article, I'll handle the rest."

Jay fell back on his bed. "God, I'll look like a fucking idiot."

"For me?"

"Only for you."

"Perfect. Now, I need you to reach out to Erick the Red and find out if he knows anything."

CHAPTER FOUR

JAY NEEDED SOME weed anyway, and Erick the Red's stuff was the best. He was a little nervous to ask Erick about Fields. Erick's subjects of interest orbited around heavy metal and dope. Anything really personal or private was met with a steel wall of indifference, probably as a coping mechanism. Jay knew Fields was a customer of Erick's, but he was pretty sure Erick didn't know Jay knew, and the last thing was his weed dealer realizing he'd been spotted doing business.

Erick lived in a nice two-story across town. His father was an invalid, his mother a teacher close to retiring. They were well-to-do but didn't show it off. Erick always seemed to have money for musical equipment and sound systems, so the weed business was probably treating him pretty well. There was a story going around about how the police had raided Erick's house and took a pound of marijuana from his room while he was out one night. When he came home, he found his mother in the kitchen with a business card in her hand and a message for Erick to call the detectives in the morning. Erick didn't call. Instead, he woke up early and drove to the police department, asking to see the detectives. He was told they weren't in yet, so he waited in the lobby. After several hours, the two detectives arrived and invited him to their office. To Erick's surprise, the detectives weren't part of the drug force, they worked in larceny. Word on the street was that one of Erick's customers was going around Grigsby, breaking into houses and stealing stuff, and any information Erick could provide would be a great help, and they would conveniently forget about the weed.

Erick said he didn't know what they were talking about.

When they insisted he did, he told the detectives to arrest him.

They refused, telling him they just wanted information about the guy.

Erick demanded to either be placed into custody or given his weed back. He refused to help them at all and wouldn't give them a reason for declining.

Fifteen minutes later, Erick walked out of their offices, through the lobby—past several on-duty deputies—and out to the parking lot, all while holding a Ziplock baggie stuffed with marijuana in plain sight, and nobody batted an eye.

Of course, that story leveled Erick up to Legendary status, which only helped his credibility. Jay didn't know if the story was true, and ultimately it didn't matter. No one is untouchable, though sometimes they could be useful. With Erick, he was of no use to them, so it was probably a matter of time before the police caught up with him.

It was well after sunset by the time Jay made it over to Erick's. He pulled his beat-up old T-100 next to Erick's car. No other cars in the driveway, which meant it was a good time to come by. He grabbed a roll of twenties from the hidden compartment in the center console and locked up his truck. Erick was waiting on the porch, shirtless and shoeless, wearing faded jeans, his long red hair still wet from the shower.

"Hey man," he said, opening the door for Jay.

A hazy cloud hung close to the ceiling, the smell of weed lingering heavy in the air. "Dude . . . burning in the house now?" Jay asked.

"Mom is at a teacher's conference and Dad is my favorite customer."

Jay shut the front door behind him. "How's he doing?"

"Dying, but then aren't we all."

Jay sat on the recliner and immediately started browsing. Hundreds, maybe thousands, of CDs were lined up in rows on the floor. Most of it metal bands Jay had never heard of, though there was some jazz and even outlaw country thrown into the mix. Erick had one of the most comprehensive Johnny Cash collections he'd ever seen. Stacks of vinyl albums towered by a DJ-style turntable. Across the room was a Marshall combo amplifier and a cream Les Paul with gold hardware. The guitar was passed down to Erick from a friend who had died by overdose. It was one of his most cherished possessions.

"Ever heard of Angel Witch?" Erick asked.

Jay shook his head. "New band?"

Erick flipped through his CDs and pulled one out. He was meticulous with his music, inserting the CD into the player only after the previous disc was safely in its corresponding jewel case. Jay had asked Erick long ago why he didn't subscribe to a music streaming service, and his answer surprised him. "It's not that I don't want to, it's more that I want to enjoy this format as long as I can. That's why I never quit buying vinyl, and now look . . . it's cool to be into actual records again."

Erick pressed play on the CD player and turned the volume up a little. "These guys were part of the New Wave of British Heavy Metal I was telling you about. Without bands like this, and Diamond Head, and Blitzkrieg, and Holocaust, you wouldn't have Metallica, or your precious Mastodon."

"Hey, what's wrong with Mastodon?"

Erick sat cross-legged on the floor and started rolling a joint. "Nothing. I like *Blood Mountain*, but *Leviathan* is my favorite."

"I like *The Hunter*."

"Deluxe edition is good, with those two extra tracks.

Drummer needs to stick with drumming." Erick licked the paper on the joint, instantly making Jay feel a little queasy about sharing it. A worldwide pandemic does that to you. Things you didn't used to give two shits about suddenly become questions of life or death. Erick lit the joint and took a small hit, then passed it over to Jay. "Careful, this one is made from roaches."

Jay smiled. He knew a few people that kept their roaches. Erick held on to them, stuffed them into old camera film canisters. Then he'd let them sit, sometimes for weeks. The resin made for some powerful shit once you broke it up and rolled it. Jay took the joint and toked, the bitter smoke burning his throat. Tasted like shit, but damn would it fuck you up. "Got any hydro?" The words were more of a cough than actual speech.

Erick shook his head. "I will though. Want to wait a couple of days?"

"No." Jay realized a way he could talk about Mr. Fields. "You get your hydro from Fields?"

Erick looked at him, his eyes narrowed. "What? Do you mean that goofy dude with the tattoos? I don't get anything from him, he buys from me. How do you know him?"

"I cut his grass."

He nodded. "Weird fucker. You know he's mobbed up, right?"

Jay took another hit off the joint. "What do you mean, mobbed up?"

Erick smiled. "Like the mafia. Russian mob."

"Fields is Russian?"

"Definitely not. Accent is European, but not English or German, so possibly Czech. That area of the world has changed so much it's hard to keep track. But I know it's not German or Russian. I lived in Germany until I was fifteen. Saw the wall come down."

"Dude, how old are you?"

"Old enough. I think Fields launders money for the Russians."

"What makes you think that?"

"Things he's said. He wanted to know about currency and bitcoin, he figured I knew something about that shit, which I don't. Fuck all that computer money, darknet crap."

"But if he's not Russian, then he can't be Russian mob, right?"

Erick shrugged. "He could be working for them."

Jay nodded, taking the joint from Erick. "You think he could be like, a hitman?"

"Who knows. All I know about him is that I never have to remind him to pay me. Good customer."

Jay held his smoke, passed the joint back to Erick. He decided to take a chance. "I think he's killed someone."

Erick's jaw clenched. "Huh?"

"Remember LuCyndi Westenraadt, the girl who went missing a while back? They found her body, just had her funeral?"

"Didn't they arrest someone already?"

"No." Jay looked at his hands, forcing himself to slow down. "I think Fields had something to do with it."

"What makes you think that? Did Fields know her?"

"I don't know. I think I found something of hers in Fields' shed."

Snuffing out the joint, Erick stood and stretched. "Sounds goofy. Call the cops if you're sure about it."

"But what if Fields is mobbed up like you say? That could be dangerous."

Erick nodded. "No doubt. All I know is he's a good customer. I don't know the guy that well and would prefer not to be involved, for obvious reasons."

"Hey, I'm spit balling here, it's probably just a weird coincidence. Say, think you could burn me a CD of that Angel Witch?" Jay handed over the roll of twenties, hoping there was enough to cover the weed and the cost of the blank CD.

Erick shuffled through the roll. "I'll burn you a greatest hits. You got any Diamond Head?"

"No."

"Good stuff. I'll throw you one in as a bonus." Erick knelt and opened the guitar case next to the Les Paul, pulled out a small baggy and tossed it over to Jay. "Come by in a few days. I gotta jet, so I guess I'll be seeing you later."

On the ride home, Jay couldn't help but feel like Erick was kicking him out because of what he said about Fields. Maybe he was being paranoid, but he felt like Erick was going to tell Fields what he'd said.

That wouldn't be good.

Not one bit.

CHAPTER FIVE

JAY WOKE UP the next morning at his desk in his underwear, a line of drool hanging from his chin. His bed was still made from the day before. Sunlight streamed through the blinds, catching motes drifting in the rays. He wiped his chin with the back of his hand, then shook his mouse to wake up his computer. A list of news stories about Carmen Garcia and Timothy Rice, the missing children, filled the screen.

LuCyndi used to babysit Carmen on the weekends during her senior year. Carmen must have been just a toddler then. Carmen's mom Frannie was spending a lot of time out of town for work at the time and Luce's mother was best friends with Frannie, so Luce was the logical choice for watching the baby. Luce hated it, called it *babyshitting* duty, but Frannie paid well. People always felt sorry for Luce because of her hearing aid, which really wasn't a big deal because that's the way things had always been for her.

No matter what it was, babysitting or helping people in the neighborhood, Luce was always paid well. Besides, the babysitting gig wasn't that bad since Frannie let Luce use her pool when she was out of town. Jay, Willi, and Arty had hung out there often enough on the weekends.

That was four years ago.

Four years.

Where did the time go?

If Willi was looking for a connection between

LuCyndi's death and Carmen, that was it. Luce was Carmen's babysitter. There was a real connection, but it stopped there.

Jay grabbed his phone and texted Willi. *What time we doing this, babe?*

Breakfast was an untoasted pop tart and orange juice. Jay regretted that combo when he brushed his teeth. He shaved and showered and combed his wet hair back. His best dress shirt, a button-down light blue oxford was clean, but looked like he had been keeping it balled up in his glove box. It took him a few minutes to figure out how to turn the iron on, then he almost burned the shirt as soon as he started.

After tucking in his shirt, he realized he didn't own a belt.

His best dress socks had so many holes his toes poked through and his dress shoes were too tight.

There was an unidentifiable stain on his khakis that wasn't going anywhere any time soon. Jay hated to consider exactly what could have made the stain, and the area felt sticky. Probably best not think about it at all.

The day hadn't even really started and already it was turning into a shitshow.

Willi finally texted back an hour later. *Pick me up at the cemetery.*

She was visiting LuCyndi's grave. Jay immediately felt guilty for not visiting the cemetery since the funeral. Chances were Willi hadn't been there either, but she had an excuse with school. Jay didn't have any excuses.

On my way.

Jay checked himself out in the mirror. Despite how ridiculous he felt wearing nice clothes, he had to admit he looked good. Well, not good, but presentable. Maybe it was time to get out there and get serious about things. Even creepy-ass Fields was right . . . he needed a job with benefits. It was time to dust off his resume and find gainful employment. Fuck school, fuck cutting grass. If he had a job, then he could save some money, and maybe even get a loan.

Get a car.

He had his truck, but it didn't look like Mr. Murray was going to get his youngest daughter a car anytime soon. Wasn't Mr. Murray's fault . . . his job had severely cut his hours back. He was hanging on by a thread, but weren't they all?

Hanging on by a thread was the only thing Jay knew. It was real, something he could touch, and maybe that's what life was all about, simply getting by.

But if Jay could get a loan, then he'd be able to get Willi a car, and he really wanted to do something for Willi, to show he could hold his own, to show he could do a little more than just get by.

The air was crisp, definitely long-sleeve weather. Jay drove in silence, the sound of the road the only thing keeping him company. It took him a few minutes to find LuCyndi's gravesite once he reached the cemetery. After driving down the wrong path twice, he finally spied Willi kneeling on the grass next to Luce's headstone. He parked and walked over.

Flower petals were scattered all over the grass. The dirt near Luce's headstone was supposed to be freshly packed. The funeral was two weeks ago, so maybe some grass sprouts would be showing, but now the ground looked like someone had tried to dig up Luce's grave.

"What happened?"

Willi looked at him. She had clearly been crying. "The groundskeeper said vandals. Sometime last night. I'm going to have to get more flowers."

"Vandals? You mean like someone deliberately singled out her grave or just some randos out fucking around?"

Willi shrugged. "They didn't see anyone, so who knows."

"You don't think it was the police? Maybe they need to look at her body again?"

"No. You need permission from a judge for exhumation, and Luce's mom would have to sign off on it too. Something like that would have made the news, we would have known."

"Why would someone do this?" Luce was one of the most popular girls at school. She had her issues with a certain Samantha Horton in junior high, but that was water under the bridge. Samantha was even at Luce's funeral.

The entire town went to Luce's funeral.

He couldn't think of anyone who would have vandalized her grave for any reason. It didn't make any sense.

Willi put her hand on Luce's headstone and whispered something to her best friend. Jay looked around, wanting something to do with his hands other than shoving them in his pockets. He didn't want to be there, but not because Willi was talking to Luce. Death always made him feel uncomfortable, graveyards even more so. He knew the cemetery shouldn't creep him out. If there was one thing that was certain about life, it was that it was destined to end, but being so close to it, so close to the evidence of death . . . it was more than a reminder for Jay.

It felt like an omen, so the further away he was from it, and the further away Willi was from it, the better.

Finally, Willi stood up and brushed the leaves from her slacks. Jay walked over to her and hugged her. She rested her head on his shoulder, and they stood like that for a few minutes, not talking, just listening to each other breathe.

"I miss her so much," Willi said.

"I know."

She raised her head and looked at Jay. "Promise me we'll get some flowers for her today, okay?"

"Sure."

She walked over to his truck. "At least you smell good."

Jay looked down at his clothes. "Hey, I put a lot of effort into this. I even ironed my shirt."

"You forgot your belt."

"I don't have a belt."

Willi grinned. "I know what I'm getting you for Christmas now."

Jay opened the door for her. "All I want for Christmas is you."

Willi kissed him on the nose. "You got it. And a belt."

While they drove to Saint Thomas Cathedral, Willie went over her strategy. "Let me do all the talking, okay? One, I don't want her to suspect you don't work for the Gazette, and two, you might say something that upsets her."

"Like what?"

"I don't know. We have to be careful. She's already reluctant, and the last thing we need is for her to kick us out."

"What are you going to ask her?"

"I have some questions."

Jay grinned. "I know that. I guess I'm curious how you're going to get her talking about all the things she said she wasn't going to talk about. What's your plan?"

Willi shook her head. "I don't know. We play it by ear and see what happens."

"You don't really have a plan. Okay, got it."

The church office next to the cathedral used to be a school administration building. Jay remembered there used to be a school there years ago. Boys in their navy pants and white short-sleeved shirts, girls in their knee-length skirts and white socks. Just like everything else in Grigsby, the school went the way of the dodo from lack of funding.

Inside, several older women sat at a table folding church bulletins. They didn't even look up when Willi and Jay walked past them. Frannie Garcia's office was on the right, her nameplate displayed on the door. Frannie sat behind the desk, speaking quietly into the phone. A pretty woman with long dark hair streaked with strands of grey,

Frannie's eyes gave away the pain she was going through. She waved them in, pointing at the chairs in front of her desk, and quickly ended her call.

After hanging up, Frannie rubbed her eyes with the heels of her hands, then looked up, smiling brightly. "How can I help you?"

Willi held out her hand. "I'm Willi Murray from the Grigsby Gazette."

Frannie's smile faded. She leaned over and shook Willi's hand. "Ah yes, about the fundraiser. I pretty much said all I'm going to say about it, so I don't know why they sent you here."

"I was hoping to get a statement from you about the search."

Frannie's eyebrows went up. "I didn't send that info in the email?" She stared at her laptop for a few seconds before clicking some things with her mouse. "I think I . . . well . . . " Frannie shook her head. "I'm sorry, guess I was wrong. What can I tell you about it?"

Willi took out her phone and opened the recording app. "I'd like to know about the time and date of the search, the area being covered, all the important information, but also . . . I'd like to know how you feel about the search."

"How do *I* feel about it?"

Willi nodded.

Frannie pursed her lips. "'Feel' is a heavy word. I . . . I honestly don't know. I guess I'm thinking that maybe we shouldn't have these kind of searches. There's never a good reason to have to search to find a missing child, ever. I know . . . times change and all that, and people are mean and cruel, but this used to be a good place. We didn't have to lock our doors at night. Everyone knew each other. Grigsby didn't have the drug problem it does now. Those times are gone, but there's no reason things couldn't be like they were, just like there's no good reason to ever have to search for your kids. So, we do what the police won't do. Not that they aren't doing their jobs, I'm not saying that at all. They're doing what they can, but it isn't enough. Kicking people out of the park isn't going to help, so we hit the streets, search in the fields, in the alleys and the woods, and we pound on doors, and we talk to anyone and everyone just in case someone might know something. And then we do it all over again."

Willi nodded. "What should people do if they think they know something?"

"They should call the hotline we set up. Anything, no matter how trivial, could help."

Willi turned off her recorder. "I think I've got it. Mind if we get a photo?"

Frannie's eyes lit up. "Oh wow, I look like shit. You know what, screw it. This isn't a time to look glamorous."

Jay used his phone and took several quick shots of Frannie.

When Willie went to stand, Frannie looked at her with a weak smile on her face. "You're LuCyndi's friend? She used to babysit Carmen."

Willi nodded.

"You two were close, right? I can't imagine what you're going through."

"I feel the same about you. This must be like hell."

Frannie tapped her pen on her desk. "It is hell. I don't remember the last time I slept. Every time the phone rings I think it's . . . "

"I'm sorry," Willie said, "I didn't mean to pry."

"No, no, no . . . I just don't want this to turn into some kind of circus with the media. But I *need* to talk about her, about Carmen. You're not prying. If anyone's doing that it's me. Carmen isn't dead, she's just . . . lost. Missing sounds so final, but lost things are always found, right?"

"Yes."

"We will find her. This search, this fundraiser to help out Mr. Rice, this is how we do it. As a community. The police have done what they can, now it's our turn. I know LuCyndi wasn't as fortunate, and it breaks my heart, but the only thing I have left is my broken heart, and the only way I can survive is to have hope and faith. And I know LuCyndi is with my Carmen right now, helping her find her way back."

Willi stared at Frannie, confusion in her eyes. "I'm sorry . . . "

Frannie smiled. "Carmen told me. Before the monster took her from me, she told me about a lady in the park, dressed all in white. She said it was Miss LuCyndi."

Jay looked at Willi, then at Frannie.

Willi sat up in her chair. "Carmen saw LuCyndi in the park? Like before they found her—"

"No. After. LuCyndi came back for Carmen after she died. She's her guardian angel. I know that now. That's why you're here, her friend, to remind me that my Carmen is safe. She is lost, but she is safe, and Miss LuCyndi will bring her back to me."

CHAPTER SIX

WILLI DIDN'T TALK when they got back in Jay's truck. They rode in silence for a while, absorbing what Frannie had told them about LuCyndi. Jay kept glancing at her, hoping to see something other than the blank expression she'd been wearing since leaving Frannie's office

Willi turned on the stereo, then turned it off. "How well do you know Gerald Rice?"

Jay looked at her. "Nope. I'm not going to—"

"Listen. All that stuff Frannie said about Luce . . . there's a connection, I feel it."

"Are you even listening to yourself? That woman is going insane wondering what the hell happened to her daughter. Her mind is mixed up, and she might not be in a good place right now. In fact, I'm pretty damn sure she's not in a good place right now. And then she starts with this paranormal mumbo jumbo and now you're getting sucked into it. C'mon Willi, since when do you believe in any of that shit?"

"This is real."

Jay pulled over on the shoulder of the road and put his truck in park. He turned and faced Willi. She stared at the road, refusing to look at Jay. He could tell she was mad. "I get it," Jay said, keeping his voice low and measured. "It feels like just yesterday Luce was here with us, and because it was so recent, so close, it just can't feel like any of this is happening, right? Like when I saw her shirt in Fields' shed, the first thing I thought was, if that's her shirt, then what

41

shirt is she wearing now? So, I get it. It hurts. It's going to hurt forever, and the only thing time is going to do is dull the pain, but it will never go away."

Willi took a deep breath and held it for a second before speaking. "If you think saying something even halfway close to what I'd say to you is going to help me through this, you are seriously fucking wrong. For the record, I don't know what I believe when it comes to that kind of stuff. I'm not into church, or religion, or whatever the fuck it is, but I also don't pretend to have all the answers." She rubbed her face with both hands. "Do I think Luce came back from the dead as a ghost to be Carmen's guardian angel? Of course not. But *something* is going on here. There's a connection, and it's driving me crazy. Maybe Mr. Rice knows something. Maybe Timothy said something, anything, and maybe it's something the police haven't made public because they don't see a connection."

"That's entirely possible."

Willi looked at Jay. "Then let's go talk to Mr. Rice. If I'm right, then maybe we'll be that much closer to finding out who killed Luce."

Jay stared back at Willi for a few seconds. At last, he lowered his head. "I haven't talked to Gerald Rice ever since Phil died. We weren't that close . . . we hung out, smoked a little weed every once in a while, but once Phil started doing the meth, I kept my distance. Mr. Rice knows me and Phil got high. He knows. What if he blames me for what happened to Phil?"

"Phil had problems long before y'all hung out. Don't you think he knows that?"

Willi did have a point. "Maybe. Maybe not. What am I going to say to him?"

"As little as possible. If he doesn't talk, then it was a wasted trip. But if he does, then he might have something to say that we don't already know."

Jay put his truck in gear and drove back onto the road. "Only one way to find out."

THE SMALL HOURS

Gerald Rice lived in a small two-bedroom house on the other side of Grigsby.

The poor side of Grigsby.

The land of trailer parks and run-down secondhand stores. Near the highway, there was an abandoned apartment complex that used to be a movie theater back in the day. That's where the police found Phil Rice. Dead in a dirty bathtub. The toxicology report listed meth and other assorted drugs. Before Phil discovered meth, he was Grigsby High's star quarterback. College scouts were already showing interest, and it seemed inevitable that great things were going to happen for him.

Great things.

Phil's father had gotten the short end of the stick his whole life. Gerald's wife Candace died young from cancer. He remarried, and that new bride took Gerald to the cleaners. He did manage to get full custody of their son, Timothy, in the divorce.

Then Phil died.

Now Timothy was missing.

Jay wondered how Gerald was feeling about things right now.

Probably not that fucking good.

Gerald was on his porch sitting in his rocking chair, smoking a cigarette and drinking a beer. When Jay pulled into the driveway, he waved at Gerald, but Gerald didn't even acknowledge him.

Jay and Willi walked up to the porch. "Hey, Gerald," Jay said.

Gerald just nodded.

"Wanted to see how you were holding up."

Gerald shrugged his shoulders and took a sip of beer. He hit a hard drag off his cigarette then crushed it out under his boot.

There were a lot of cigarette butts on the porch.

"Suppose you're here to gloat," Gerald said.

Jay stepped up on the porch. "I'm sorry."

"Surprised you didn't pass Barnes on your way up here."

Jay shook his head. "I just wanted to check on you. I didn't see anyone else on the way here."

Gerald reached into his cooler and grabbed another beer. "That's nice of you. Very thoughtful. Come check on the local fuck up. See for yourself, then the bullshit spreads, right?"

"Gerald, what are you talking about?"

Gerald swigged his beer. "You mean you don't know?" he said, his voice laced with bitterness.

"About what?"

Gerald shrugged. "Barnes just left here. They found . . . they found my boy. Two down, none left. They want me to go by the morgue to identify the remains. That's what he called my boy . . . my Timothy. Remains. Guess we don't have to go around looking for him anymore, now that they found his *remains*."

Willi moaned behind Jay. He looked back at her, watched her fighting back tears. "Gerald, honest . . . I didn't know. Oh my God, I . . . I'm sorry. I—"

"Sorry. *SORRY!*" Gerald's scream sounded all through the block. "You're sorry? Goddammit all to hell son, what the fuck do *you* have to be sorry about? Sorry . . . you don't even fucking know."

Jay backed off the porch. "Listen . . . I had no idea. I just wanted to check on you, that's all."

Gerald nodded. He smiled weakly, drained his beer then dropped the empty on the porch by his chair. "I know, I know. Appreciate it. Come back anytime. We'll kick back and drink a few, right . . . talk about all the bullshit."

"I'm sorry, seriously."

Gerald lit another cigarette. He stared off in the distance. "Well, y'all take care now. I got to be going to the morgue in a few."

Back in the truck, Jay's hands trembled on the steering wheel. Willi looked out the window, occasionally sobbing.

THE SMALL HOURS

Jay drove to Mae's Diner and pulled into the back of the parking lot.

"I'm not hungry," Willi said.

"Oh, we're not eating." Jay opened his console and took out his bag of weed and rolling papers.

Willi side-eyed him. "Really? Here?"

Jay licked the joint and dug out his lighter from his pocket. "Yes, here. I don't give a fuck right now."

Willi normally didn't like getting high. The few times Jay could remember smoking with her she had taken a couple of hits and conked out for hours. Today though, as soon as the aroma of the weed hit her nostrils, she held her hand out. "Yep, fuck it. Gimme some of that."

Jay passed her the joint. "Hope you don't have anything to do for the next few hours."

Willi hit it and coughed. "Tomorrow . . . security cameras."

"We could do it today?"

Willi looked at Jay, her eyes already bloodshot. "Tomorrow."

They didn't say anything until he dropped her back off at her house.

Willi grabbed her purse. "I'm sorry."

"For what?"

"Asking you to go to Mr. Rice's house."

"Don't. You didn't know."

Jay squeezed her shoulder. Willi leaned back on him, resting her head on his chest. "If Timothy's body has been found . . . "

Jay shushed her. "This is bad. This is so fucking bad."

Willi nodded. "It's about to get worse."

"God, I hope you're wrong."

CHAPTER SEVEN

THE NEWS SPREAD FAST, and by the next morning, it was the main story on the local news. No leads, curfew heavily enforced, any tips or leads please call, operators were standing by. They actually said that. Detective Barnes, sweating in his suit despite the cool temperatures, offered only condolences and promises of justice at the press conference. Details were scarce, but from what Jay could gather, Timothy Rice's body was discovered in a drainage canal miles away from the park. He was identified by his clothes. One article said his throat was torn out; another said what was left of his body was unrecognizable. The police were still going with the deranged homeless person in the park theory because they didn't have anything else to go on. Jay was surprised Barnes hadn't mentioned meth during the presser, but he knew that was what was going through Barnes' head.

According to Barnes, drugs were the root of all evil, and he was on a one-man crusade to stamp all the drugs out of Grigsby, even the demonic reefer. It was all just a bunch of talk to keep the conservatives happy and contributing to their efforts.

Willi walked over to Jay's house early, wearing ripped-up jeans and an old long-sleeved flannel shirt. If they were to pull this off, they needed to look the part. To check for surveillance at Fields' house, they should probably actually be doing a little yard work so the neighbors wouldn't get suspicious. Mrs. Teller was likely the only one who would notice them. No one else on the block paid attention to anything, totally oblivious to the serial killer living among them. And if Fields did have security cameras, then at least he'd think they were just cleaning up his yard.

Jay's mom was already out and about that morning, so they had the place to themselves. Willi used the key under the mat and let herself in, sneaking through the hallway to Jay's bedroom, hoping to surprise him in bed.

Instead, Jay was sitting in his underwear at his desk, staring at his computer screen. He was reading a page from the local news website. He looked over at Willi when she opened his door, motioning with his eyes for her to check out what he was reading. "This shit is terrible."

Willi frowned. "Reading about it isn't going to fix it. We need to do something."

"We are. Quinten's coming by later to discuss the game plan."

"I'm overjoyed."

Jay scowled at Willi. "Getting him involved was your idea."

"I know, I know. I just hope he doesn't, like . . . try to control everything."

"Have you ever broken into a house?"

Willi sat down on Jay's bed. "Of course not."

"He has. If anyone can control the situation, it's Quinten." Jay closed the browser and stood. "I need a shower and some breakfast."

"A shower? We're about to go to Fields' house and act like we're cleaning out his gutters."

Jay laughed. "I don't plan on doing any actual work."

Willi hung her head down. "You're like . . . *the* worst. What if someone sees us?"

"We *act* like we're working. This isn't even going to take fifteen minutes."

"Not if we don't want to look like we're snooping around. If someone sees us, which they probably will, then we need to put on a little show . . . like clean up a little."

"Sure. Okay, I get what you're saying. But I need to eat."

After Jay dressed, they left his room and started cooking breakfast. Jay handled the biscuits and bacon while Willi scrambled eggs. Jay's mom had killed most of the coffee before she left so they brewed another pot. Jay liked his scrambled eggs cooked in the leftover bacon grease while Willi preferred a cleaner approach, with a little milk and a small amount of butter. When they finished, Jay had a heaping pile of scrambled eggs on his plate while Willi's omelets looked like something you'd see on a cooking show. "Those eggs are going to wreck your gut," Willi said, chewing on a slice of bacon.

Jay thumped his belly. "This sculpted thing? Cast iron baby, nothing can hurt it."

"Sculpted my ass. You might have abs in there somewhere, but I don't believe you've ever stumbled across a sit-up in your life."

"Whoa, what's with all the trash talk? Not this early in the morning."

After breakfast, they cleared the table and cleaned the dishes, then set off to Fields' house. The house was the center home in a cul-de-sac, and even though they were next-door neighbors, it was still a little walking distance. Jay kept his yardwork gear in his truck. Willi went to Jay's truck and waded through all the junk shoved behind the bench seat until she found a pair of gloves and protective goggles. Jay grabbed a roll of large black garbage bags and pulled a couple off the roll. Willi caught his eye and nodded behind her. Sure enough, the family across the street from Fields' house was having a garage sale, and people were just starting to show up. They were going to have to make this look good.

Jay walked across the yard and stepped onto Fields' driveway with confidence, like he had every right to be there. He even waved at the people at the sale.

"What the fuck are you doing?" Willi said through a fake smile.

"Looking normal."

"Yes, we want to look normal, but there's no need to make yourself easily identifiable by people you don't even know."

Jay shook his head. "Dammit, we're going to have to actually work."

"Told you."

While picking up broken branches and twigs in the yard, Jay looked all around the front of the house for anything that looked like it could be a camera. Nothing obvious stood out, but that didn't mean Fields hadn't installed something that wouldn't look like a camera at first glance. Jay checked the front door, above the door jamb, around the doorknob, even the peephole. Next, he looked all around the mailbox mounted by the door, and the three plants on the porch near the front door.

Nothing.

He joined Willi in the backyard. She was working around the shed, filling the garbage bag with leaves, sneaking looks at the padlock and door, and all around the roof of the building. Jay checked the rear door, all around the gutters along the roofline, even in the old rusted out barbecue pit that longed for the dumpster.

They found nothing out of the ordinary. As far as they could tell, Fields did not have any type of surveillance around his house. Of course, that didn't definitely mean none existed, it only meant they were unable to find it.

"We have to assume he has something," Willi said, spinning her garbage bag shut.

Jay nodded, pointing to the padlock on the door to the shed. "We need to make sure to bring something to cut that lock."

"There's a window on the other side, we could get in that way."

Sure enough, there was a window on the far side of the shed. Jay tugged at the bottom of the window. "I think it's locked."

"Quit pulling on it in the broad daylight," Willi said, keeping her voice down. "We may have to break it, but it beats cutting through a padlock." She wrinkled her nose. "Is he storing paint in there?"

Jay nodded. "There's a bunch of spray paint cans in a bucket in the back."

Willi sniffed the air, her nostrils flaring. "Yep, I smell the paint, but there's something else."

A car playing loud music turned onto the street. Jay and Willi stepped around to the front of the shed and listened. The sound was closer now. Heavy metal guitars, pounding drums, a chorus of women shouting *1 . . . 2 . . . 3 . . . 4 . . . what are we living for . . .*

"Who the hell is that?" Willi said.

Jay listened as the music continued to play. "It's some girl band. The Runaways?"

Willi laughed. "No, it's not the Runaways." She listened for a second, then grinned. "Girlschool," she said, nodding, "Yep, that's definitely Girlschool."

The music ended abruptly as the car shut off. "Whoever it is, they pulled in the driveway."

From the backyard, Jay could see through the windows into the living room. Either Fields forgot to lower his blinds, or he didn't have anything in the house that he minded people seeing. The front door opened, and a trio of women walked into the house. They were talking, all at once, and Jay couldn't make out what they were saying. "It's the cleaning service."

Willi squinted, trying to get a better look through the window. "Weirdest looking cleaning service I've ever seen."

Jay had never really paid attention to the women that came over to Fields' house. He had assumed they worked for a service, but now that he had a better look at them, he wasn't so sure. They weren't wearing uniforms, just skimpy tops with short skirts that barely covered anything.

"They look like hookers," Willi said.

"Hey now."

"Well, sorry . . . they do."

"They could be dancers that also work for a cleaning service."

Willi nodded. "Maybe, or they could just be strippers that like to hang out at a weird European guy's house during the day."

"They have a key, so they either know Fields or they work for a cleaning service."

They watched the women walk by the kitchen. If they saw Jay and Willi standing in the backyard staring at them, they didn't acknowledge it. One of the women was Latina, the other white, while the third appeared to be Asian. The white woman was tall with streaks of lavender through her long golden locks. She went to the refrigerator and removed a bottle of water. The Latina girl uncorked a bottle of wine while the Asian girl put three glasses on the counter. The blonde was talking, but neither Jay nor Willi could hear what she was saying.

"We better go," Willi said.

Jay picked up the garbage bags full of leaves and branches and placed them in the front near the curb while Willi took off her gloves and shoved them into the back pocket of her jeans. The car in the driveway was a bright green Mustang with a series of long scratches down the passenger side. Jay pointed at the car and looked at Willi. "Looks like they drive like you do," he said, laughing.

Willi shot him the finger and walked through the grass back to Jay's house.

Whoever these women were, cleaners or sex workers, Jay and Willi didn't want to be seen in Fields' backyard any longer.

CHAPTER EIGHT

UINTEN WAS ON board with breaking into Fields' shed, but he was more interested in what Jay told him about Erick the Red. "How'd you meet Erick?"

Jay knew where he was going with this. "C'mon man."

"Dude, everyone knows you went to see a therapist."

Willi looked over at Jay. "Therapist?"

"Not everyone," Jay said. Quinten was what Jay thought of as a 'lovable asshole' . . . no matter how shitty he was, you couldn't stay mad at him. Opening his mouth and inserting his foot was just Quinten being Quinten, and they were all used to it.

"You went to therapy?" Willi said, her eyes wide.

"Well, *now* everyone knows. Okay, no big deal." Quinten smiled. "Jay knows Erick because they have the same therapist, and I know because she's my therapist too."

Now it was Jay and Willi that stared at Quinten. "You're in therapy?" they both said in unison.

"Hey, if I wasn't, years from now y'all would be yelling from the rooftops that I should have gone to therapy. I get frustrated with things. I've got anger management issues. Stress."

"Stress? You're twenty years old," Jay said.

"And I'm the youngest salesperson on the floor too. Big shoes to fill."

"You're the one who wanted that job in the first place. Why not do something that's less taxing?" Jay asked.

"Yes, why be a slimy car salesman?" Willi added, pouring a little fuel on the fire.

Quinten wasn't taking the bait. He rubbed his fingertips together, nodding. "Money, baby."

Willi rolled her eyes. "You've been there a year. Made a hundred grand yet?"

"No, but I'm working on it."

"Working yourself to an early grave is more like it," Willi said. She turned her attention to Jay. "Since when?"

"Couple of months. I . . . have some things to work out. I should have told you, I'm sorry."

Willi leaned over and hugged Jay. "Nothing to be sorry about, I just wish I would have known. But, hey . . . maybe I should start therapy too."

"Group is about to get *really* interesting," Quinten said, winking at Willi.

"Not on your life, and especially not with you," she said to Quinten. "Who's this therapist?"

"Dr. Jo? She's . . . well, she's something else," Jay said. "I had all these ideas of what therapy was supposed to be like, all that crappy shit you see on TV, and it's nothing like that. We just . . . talk. It's a conversation, questions and answers. And scenarios."

Quinten nodded. "*Yes!* Her scenarios are fucking awesome."

"Scenarios?" Willi looked seriously perplexed.

"Like, she presents frustrating real-life situations. It's controlled role-playing, and you can break character whenever it gets too uncomfortable. She builds these scenarios after getting to know you, that way it's not some generic situation, but something you'd actually encounter."

"So, scenarios with meds?"

"No. She doesn't like chemicals unless it's absolutely necessary."

"Dr. Jo did her doctoral study on over-medication," Quinten added.

"How do you know Erick the Red sees her?" Willi asked.

"I've seen him there," Quinten said, "so either he's selling her weed or he's in therapy."

"Erick was no help," Jay said, explaining how Erick had all but clammed up when he started asking questions about Fields. "It's weird because Erick's the one who brought Fields up in the first place. Said he was mobbed up."

Quinten began counting off on his fingers, "Fields is Russian mafia, probably a hitman, you think you saw LuCyndi's shirt in his shed, and Fields is out of town, so you want to break into his shed to take pictures of the shirt. We got breaking and entering, stalking, trespassing . . . am I missing anything?"

"Nope, that's enough there for multiple felonies," Willi said.

"Cool. I'm in."

"Now all we need is Arty and we're good," Jay said.

"Yeah . . . about Arty," Quinten said.

The last anyone had seen of Arty was at LuCyndi's funeral. He was a pallbearer, but you could see it in his eyes . . . he was barely there. With the exception of a few phone calls, no one had spoken to him since then. He quit his classes, quit going to work, and the last anyone knew of him was he was rarely leaving the house. If anyone needed therapy, it was probably Arty. Jay was ashamed he hadn't done more to reach out to him, but felt like he also needed to give Arty his space.

"Has anyone talked to him?" Willi asked.

Jay shrugged. "I dropped the ball."

"It's not like he's trying anyway," Quinten added. "I mean, let's be fair. We've all tried to talk to him, he just doesn't want to engage."

Jay pulled his phone out of his back pocket. He tapped out a text message and hit send. "Guess we'll find out."

Willi tried to grab Jay's phone from him, but he moved his hand out of reach. "What did you text him?"

THE SMALL HOURS

"Do you want to catch LuCyndi's killer?"

"Jay!"

Quinten laughed. "That'll get his attention." He reclined in Jay's chair. "We need flashlights, rope, and a knife."

"A knife?" Willi said.

"That's my go-to survival kit."

"Sounds like something you bring with you to get in and out of Walmart," Willi said.

Jay knelt on the floor and reached under his bed. He pulled out a dusty duffel bag and unzipped it. "Gotcha covered," he said, tossing a flashlight over to Quinten. He pulled out a length of rope, some duct tape, and a hunting knife in a leather sheath.

"What the fuck?" Willi said.

"We need to be prepared."

"With a knife? We're not going to kill anyone. Pictures, remember? We need a camera."

Quinten pulled a small digital camera from his front pocket. "Takes better pictures in low light than that Apple crap."

"A cardboard box with a hole in it takes better pictures than any iPhone," Jay said.

Willi leaned in close. "Listen up guys. Let's not make this too complicated. In and out, right? We get in the easiest way possible, take the pictures, and get the hell out of there."

"You're making it sound like a three-minute job," Jay said, "there's a fucking padlock on the door. We're going to have to cut it or pry it off. Or break the window on the side of the shed without waking up everyone in the neighborhood."

"We need to make this look like a real break-in," Quinten added.

Willi nodded. "Right, which is why I got these." She held up a handful of medical gloves.

"Where did you find those?" Jay asked.

"My aunt hooked me up."

Quinten's eyes narrowed. "Last couple of years nobody could get their hands on gloves, masks, hand sanitizer, fucking toilet paper . . . for months . . . and your aunt's been hoarding that shit?"

"She's. A. Nurse," Willi said.

Quinten held up his hands. "Just saying . . . " He put the digital camera back in his pocket. "You're positive Fields has left town?"

Willi nodded. "From the looks of it."

"Then we do this tonight."

"Tonight?" Willi asked.

Quinten picked up the flashlight and turned it on. "You want to wait until he's pulling in the driveway?" He turned off the flashlight. "Things happen, plans change, and home is always closer than you think it is. He could be on his way back right now. No better time than the present."

Jay held up his phone, smiling. "Got a reply."

"From Arty?" Willi asked.

"Yep. He said, *'Fuck yeah!'*"

PART TWO:

THIS ANNIHILATION

CHAPTER NINE

THEY DECIDED TO meet at Quinten's house at 11:30 pm. Quinten's dad worked night shifts, so Quinten pretty much had the house to himself. Jay had texted Arty instructions on where to meet, what to wear, things he needed to bring—basically just a flashlight—and what time. Arty had texted back *I'm there* and that was the last Jay had heard from him.

It was 11:40 and there was no sign of Arty.

Quinten smoked a cigarette in the unlit garage, complaining about Jay showing up stoned. Dressed head-to-toe in black, Quinten looked like a ninja. He'd even smeared black paint on his face. "Can't believe you smoked a bowl before this. We all need clear heads tonight."

Jay, dressed in dingy grey twill pants and an old turtleneck sweater, played it off. "Dude, I'm fucking nervous. And it was a joint, not a bowl."

"Whatev, same thing."

Willi drank from a water bottle. "Where's Arty?"

"Don't know. He said he was in, but . . . "

"We ride in ten minutes," Quinten said.

Jay laughed. "You're acting like we're breaking into Fort Knox."

Quinten unzipped the duffle bag at his feet and pulled out a crowbar. "I've got bolt-cutters too, just in case. And no, this isn't going to take ten minutes. This will probably take longer than you think because we haven't thought of everything that can and will go wrong."

"What can go wrong?" Willi asked.

"Getting caught, for starters." He pointed at the back of his truck. "Everyone put your phones on the tailgate."

"Do what?" Jay asked.

"You want the police to have proof we were at Fields' house if something goes south? The less of a trackable signal we leave, the better off we are."

They all put their phones on the tailgate.

Quinten looked down the street. "Head's up, someone's coming." He put his hand on the bottom of the garage door, ready to pull it down in case whoever was walking down the street paid them any attention.

Jay watched the figure approach. After a few seconds, he looked back to Quinten, smiling. "Chill, it's Arty."

Arty walked up the drive, dressed in black training pants and a tight Lycra shirt, a black beanie snug on his head. "I was hoping y'all were still waiting on me."

Quinten stubbed his cigarette out and went over to greet Arty. "You're late, as usual," he said, giving Arty a tight hug. Arty then hugged Willi, and finally Jay. Arty looked at Jay when they'd finished hugging. "Hey, no need for waterworks."

"I'm not crying," Jay said, wiping his eyes with his sleeve.

"Bullshit. It's okay, it's cool. I've been a shitty friend."

"We've all been shitty friends," Willi said. "We all could have done better."

"I think none of us knew what to say, or how . . . " Jay said.

Arty waved them off. "Don't worry about it. I . . . could have done better too. Don't blame yourselves, because you're right. You didn't know what to say. What *can* you say? I'm the one who withdrew, clammed up, whatever you want to call it. That was probably not a good thing for me to do. I think it made things worse, but I didn't know that at the time. Wallowing around in your own shit, you think you don't need anyone else but yourself, so it's easy to stay away, but that was the last thing I should have done, and I'm sorry about that."

They all looked at their feet, nodding in agreement.

"Are you . . . good, now?" Willi asked.

He nodded. "Yeah, pretty much. I went through a lot of shit. To hell and back, as they say, but hey . . . let's get this fucker, right?"

Jay quickly explained to Arty what he had seen in Fields' shed, and what they planned to do to get the evidence they needed. "Hopefully, the police will listen."

"Fuck the police. Know how many times they've contacted me, for anything? Once. That's it. No follow-up. When I call the detective now, it goes straight to voicemail." Arty pulled out his phone. "But hey, y'all see this?" He opened the local news app and showed them his screen. "They found that girl."

Willi was about to say something, then shook her head, not saying a word.

"No no no, she's alive." Arty was quick to assure, "Everything's fine."

Willi grabbed the phone from Arty. Everyone gathered around her, looking at the photo on the screen. Carmen Garcia, her face and clothes dirty, but smiling, stood next to her mother, Frannie. Willi scrolled through the article, reading choice lines aloud. "Unharmed. Went to her own house and knocked on the door. A neighbor saw her and immediately called 911. Frannie Garcia is overjoyed, but she stressed that people should remain vigilant in finding out who killed Timothy Rice. Oh my God . . . oh God . . . "

"What?" Quinten asked.

Jay read over Willi's shoulder. "'*My daughter's guardian angel brought her back home to me.*' Frannie has this bonkers idea that LuCyndi was Carmen's guardian angel."

Willi looked at them, tears in her eyes. "The picture, look at the picture. In Carmen's hand . . . "

Jay stared at the screen. Carmen was holding

something. It took him a few seconds to realize what it was. "Holy shit."

Willi's eyes were wide. "That's Luce's hearing aid. It's got to be, right? Why would she be holding Luce's hearing aid?"

Quinten leaned over the phone, squinting. "Looks like earbuds."

Jay rubbed Willi's back. "It could be LuCyndi's. It looks like the over-the-ear kind she liked. It could be an earbud, too. Maybe Carmen found it."

Willi shook her head. "We buried it with her. Her mother requested it."

"Luce could have left one of her hearing aids at Carmen's house when she babysat her."

"That was years ago." Willi bit her lip. "But yeah, you're right. She could have forgotten it there. It could be anyone's hearing aid." She handed the phone back to Arty. After wiping her eyes on her sleeve, she stood up straight. "I'm sorry . . . this is a little too much for me."

Quinten touched Willi on her shoulder. "That's why we're doing this, together. We have each other's backs, right?"

They all nodded.

"We get in, take some pictures, get out, and get the pictures in the mail."

"That'll get their attention," Willi added.

"And if it doesn't?" Arty asked.

"Then we go on to plan B," Quinten said.

"Wait . . . what the hell is plan B? Plan A isn't good?" Jay said, shaking his head.

Quinten zipped his duffle bag shut and threw it over his shoulder. "Plan A has to fail before we can get to plan B. Let's ride."

CHAPTER TEN

JAY, WILLI, AND ARTY squeezed into Jay's truck while Quinten lay in the bed like they were on a covert reconnaissance mission. Jay parked one street over from the cul-de-sac and they walked through the alley behind the houses, staying in the shadows and taking care to make sure no one could see them. Just four friends, dressed in black, about to break into a man's shed to take pictures of a t-shirt that may or may not have belonged to a girl who'd been murdered.

Jay knew Willi was right. Her fears of breaking into Fields' shed were legitimate. This was a huge risk, one with serious consequences if things went south. Good intentions or not, they were still breaking the law. But if it meant the police would listen to them, if it meant that LuCyndi's killer would see justice, Jay felt it was worth it.

He didn't know what else to do.

He knew what he'd seen in Fields' shed. That shirt was LuCyndi's.

And now Timothy Rice was dead.

If Fields was involved in any of it, they were doing the right thing.

The moon above gave them very little light. Quinten told them not to turn their flashlights on until they were in Fields' backyard, preferably when they were safely in the shed. The streets were deserted and though it wasn't that cold, the snap in the breeze made Jay wish he'd dressed a little warmer. Willi, wearing black tights and a thin sweatshirt, had to be freezing. Every time Jay looked back at her he could see her shivering, and he could occasionally hear her teeth chattering.

When they arrived at Fields' house, Quinten checked for any signs of activity. When he returned from walking the perimeter, he gave them the all-clear and they made their way to the shed through the shadows, avoiding the bright streetlights.

Quinten quietly unzipped his duffle bag. He looked at Jay and nodded at the door to the shed. "Are you sure this is the only way in?"

Jay shrugged.

"You mean you've cut this guy's grass all summer long and you don't know?" He looked at Arty. "Do me a solid and check around back."

Arty nodded and disappeared around the back of the shed.

Quinten pulled out the crowbar. "This shed is massive. You said you think there's a metal door inside?"

"There *is* a metal door, I'm sure of it."

"Like a panic room?" Willi asked.

Quinten shook his head. "Unlikely. Not outside, too dangerous. The idea with a panic room is to be safe *inside* your house."

Arty came around from the rear of the shed. "I don't know if this is a door or not, but there's something back there that looks like it could be opened."

They made their way around the side of the shed to see what Arty was talking about. "Damn, this shed is massive," Quinten said. "It's more like an old garage that's been converted."

"Converted into what?" Jay asked. He had never paid attention to exactly how big the shed was. At first glance, the building just looked like an old rickety structure deteriorating in Fields' backyard, but now he realized it was something much more.

Quinten tapped on the wooden siding. "I think these

boards are hiding the fact that the building is made of metal."

"Why would he have a metal building in his backyard?" Willi asked, her voice rising.

Quinten motioned for her to stay quiet. "A better question is why would he *hide* a metal building in his backyard? That's what we're going to find out," he said. He grabbed the doorknob on the back of the shed and gave it a turn. Jay could tell the knob wasn't budging. There was no keyhole near the door which meant it was locked from the inside. "We're not getting in this way," Quinten said. They walked back to the front of the shed and took lookout positions while Quinten pried the padlock off the door. He tugged at the metal housing with the crowbar, moving top to bottom, then side to side, working it off the door without bending it. The wooden door was old and yielded to his prying, but the crowbar dented the wood around the housing. "I might be able to shove this back into the wood, so it'll look like no one broke in." He pulled the door open and peered inside the darkened shed. "Well, let's not all stand around like a bunch of dumbass robbers, c'mon."

They stepped into the shed and turned on their flashlights. Quinten pulled the door shut behind them. Fortunately, there were no windows, so no one would see their flashlights while they were inside. Quinten held his flashlight in his mouth, looking like the dude from the *Splinter Cell* games. Jay hated those games, couldn't get past the tutorial at the beginning. He wanted to tell Quinten he looked like a moron but decided against it. Quinten was prone to take things to the extreme, and though he looked silly, Jay was grateful he was there. If there was anyone who could be counted on to be a badass, it was Quinten.

Jay turned on his flashlight and aimed for the workbench along the wall.

Fuck.

The shirt was gone.

The snips of wire and tiny screws were still there, as well as the thin layer of dust covering everything.

Except for where the shirt had been.

There wasn't any dust there.

"Dammit," Jay said, aiming his flashlight at Willi.

"It's not here," she said.

"I swear it was right here, practically hanging off the edge. You can see where it was. There's no dust." Jay pointed the flashlight at the place where the shirt had been.

Quinten turned his attention to the workbench, still holding his flashlight with his teeth. He knelt in front of the bench, peering underneath it to see if the t-shirt had simply fallen to the floor. There wasn't anything under the bench other than an old gas generator that looked like it was straight out of the 1970s.

"It stinks in here," Willi said. Jay flashed the light at her, careful not to shine it in her eyes. He could see her nose wrinkled in disgust.

"No shit," Arty said.

"Yes shit, actually," Quinten said, "it smells like old turds in here. Chemicals too."

"It's probably those old cans of spray paint over there," Jay said, aiming his flashlight toward the hanging tarp that separated the front of the shed from the rear.

"Okay, time to go," Willi said. She turned her flashlight off and started to make her way to the entrance.

"Hey . . . hold up a sec," Quinten said. He shined his flashlight on the tarp. "We're here, right? Might as well have a look around. Like . . . " he tapped on the tarp, "what's behind this?"

"We need to get out of here," Willi said.

"Yeah," Arty added, "this place is giving me the creeps."

Jay shined his light at Arty and could see that he was having a rough time. "You all right, buddy?"

Arty nodded. "Just claustrophobic."

Quinten nodded. "Hey, it's cool. Why don't y'all go

outside, close the door, and let me look around. That way I'm the only one who could get in trouble."

"Unfortunately, the law doesn't look at it like that. Guilty by association and all that shit," Willi said.

"Not if I say I forced you into all of this," Quinten said. "Seriously, I'll take the heat for it."

Jay started to say something, but Quinten cut him off by holding up a finger. "Shhhhh, listen . . . "

Jay couldn't hear anything. Well, that wasn't exactly true. Once everyone stopped talking, it was utterly silent in the shed. He looked at Quinten, who was now holding his finger at his mouth, the universal symbol for shut-the-fuck-up.

The silence was maddening. "What?" Jay finally said, his voice barely a whisper.

"Someone's here," Quinten said. He turned off his flashlight and everyone else did the same. Jay couldn't see shit in the darkness, but he felt Willi standing next to him. He reached out for her hand and squeezed it tight. Then he heard it.

A car.

A car was running in the driveway.

Someone was talking, but Jay couldn't tell who it was, or what they were saying. The sound was distant and muffled, but there was definitely a car running in Fields' driveway.

The engine turned off.

He heard two sounds, which could have been car doors shutting.

Was it the police? Was that what he was hearing? Had someone seen them in the backyard, some do-gooding neighborhood watcher peering through their drapes?

It was probably Mrs. Teller, that old racist bitch. Jay could only imagine her call to the police, fretting about a bunch of kids prowling around. *And that colored girl too.*

Images of the next few minutes played out in Jay's imagination. Cops busting through the door, spotlights on hi-beam, K-9 patrol in full force, barking and snarling. Handcuffs, fingerprints, the inevitable mugshot that would end up in the paper. They were all getting busted. Arty, Quinten, and Willi.

Oh shit.

Willi's college career was probably fucked.

Their relationship was probably fucked.

She had told him this was a bad idea.

She'd told him it was criminal.

Jay realized he was holding his breath. He let it out slow and steady to keep from making a sound.

Footsteps.

Someone was walking up the driveway.

Voices.

Talking.

Was someone laughing?

The voices were not men.

No, one hundred percent female.

And laughing.

He couldn't hear the footsteps on the driveway anymore, but he did hear them walking through the grass, getting closer to the shed. Why were they headed there?

Whoever it was, they were definitely walking to the shed.

The door opened.

Three figures, silhouetted in the dim moonlight, stood in the doorway.

One of the figures reached towards them with long fingers outstretched, as though feeling to see if anyone was there with them in the darkness.

A bright light came on overhead. Jay watched as a tall blonde let go of the light cord.

It was the cleaning women. He sighed with relief. There was a way out of this if they played their cards right.

The brunette stepped forward, smiling. "Hello, boys, and lady."

CHAPTER ELEVEN

"**HELLO LADIES**," Quinten said, flashing his patented smile that was known to drive girls wild.

Quinten certainly had a way with women. Jay couldn't help but grin. "Hey, guess y'all decided to get some work done tonight here too. We're just finishing up with the gutters, so we'll be getting out of your hair now," Jay said, maintaining a steady, gentle voice.

"Nonsense," the brunette said, her intense stare never wavering. Jay didn't like the way she was looking at them, as though she knew something they didn't—like she was in on some private joke and they were the punchline. Maybe it was his imagination. The women didn't look like they meant any harm. The brunette was wearing a short skirt and halter top, seemingly unfazed by the cold air outside. The tall blonde woman was wearing leather pants and heels, with a short black jacket covering a skimpy top. The Asian woman stood at the back, wearing a longer shirt, leather jacket, and sunglasses.

Jay started to move closer to try to slip past them. The brunette placed her hand on his chest gently to stop him. Her hand was ice cold.

"We're not here to work," she said. "We're here to party."

"Party?" Jay said.

"Party," the blonde said. She didn't sound American. Definitely European. She shrugged the large purse off of her shoulder and set it on the ground, unzipping it and pulling out a fifth of Crown Royal, still in its velvet bag.

"Who wants to get drunk?" the brunette said, clinking shot glasses on her fingers like castanets.

Willi stepped forward. "We're all underage."

"Speak for yourself," Quinten said, reaching for one of the shot glasses.

Jay cleared his throat. "Yes, we're underage. Wouldn't want anyone to get in trouble."

The Asian woman at the rear spoke up. "Trouble?"

"Contributing to the delinquency of a minor," Arty said. "They could charge you with that."

The Asian woman laughed. "Who's going to charge us?"

"Yeah, who?" said the brunette. "It's only us party animals here."

Quinten put his hand down. He cocked his head and stuck a finger in his ear, wiggling it vigorously like he was digging out an earache. "Um, yeah . . . on second thought, probably best we get going."

An icepick of pain stabbed Jay's forehead. He glanced over at Willi and saw her wincing. Jay looked back at the brunette and felt it again.

Something wasn't right.

"The door," said the blonde woman, pointing at the tarp hanging across the room.

"The door?" Jay said. His words felt sluggish, like his tongue wasn't working.

"It's locked," Quinten said. It was obvious he was feeling out of sorts as well. His eyes were crying as he clenched his jaw.

The brunette held up a set of keys. "Nothing's locked in here. You came here to see what's behind the door, right?"

"No, we're just clearing the gutters out," Jay said.

"It's okay. We came here to see as well," she said, "we want to know what's behind the door." She jingled the keys in front of Quinten's face. "My name is Monica. The tall beauty before you is Mikayla, and the dark and sultry one behind her is Flo."

THE SMALL HOURS

"A little bit of Monica in my life, a little Mikayla to be my wife, Flo along for the ride." Quinten slicked his hair back, still trying to win the ladies over.

Willi laughed. "We really don't care what's behind the door. The gutters are clear enough for now, and I have to get back to my mom's, she's expecting me. Y'all want to check it out, no problem."

Jay made a move to slip past them again, gripping Willi's hand, but Monica slid in front of him. He didn't remember her being so close to him before, but now she was right there, less than a foot away. He never even saw her move.

"The door is behind you. We have the key, and since the rat's away . . . time to play."

"You mean, cat's away . . . right?" Quinten said.

"Cat?" Mikayla said, giggling. "Fields is certainly no cat."

"You heard me right the first time," Monica said, "I said rat, and I meant it. Fuck that goofy bastard. We know there's a key to that door on this ring, and we're not leaving until the door is open. You're not either."

"You can't keep us here," Arty said. Jay looked over his shoulder at Arty, who was visibly unwell as a result of whatever was afflicting them. His face was pale, and he looked like he was going to puke.

"You're our insurance. That way, when slimy little Fields thinks someone's been inside his precious garage and secret room, we can say it was you."

"That's bullshit," Quinten said, clenching his fists. Jay felt his heartbeat quicken. His nerves were wrecked, but he was glad Quinten was beginning to see how serious the situation was becoming. They had to get out of there.

"Calm down big boy. If you stick around, we'll say nothing. Besides, it's not like we're going to touch anything in there, we'll just take a look around. There's probably nothing in there anyway. Bunch of dusty old things."

"Like what?" Jay asked.

"Boxes, old furniture, clothes. Probably a bunch of dirty magazines, knowing Fields."

Jay knew that Willi really wanted to get in that back room. He did too. This was their only chance. If Fields was hiding something in the shed, he'd have it under lock and key. There *had* to be something in there. In totally different circumstances, Jay would have probably tried to break into the back room. But now, with the women there, he was hesitant. They probably didn't suspect Fields of murder. Maybe they thought he was hiding drugs or money. Or jewels. With them there, Jay had a bad feeling he couldn't put his finger on.

The women slid past them and pulled the tarp back to get to the door. "Stand back men, let the women handle this."

"I'm not a man," Willi said.

Flo turned and looked at her. "You might as well be, afraid of your own shadow."

Monica was working on the lock, trying out different keys. "Fucking Fields, always changing the locks. Such a rat."

Jay watched her, slowly backing away toward the shed's front entrance, pulling Willi with him. Mikayla looked back at them and the door slammed shut behind him.

Probably the wind.

"Got it," Monica said, "third key was the charm."

"Trinity," Mikayla said.

"Yes, yes, trinity."

Monica turned the doorknob and opened the door. Immediately, the odor from inside the room hit Jay's nostrils. It was foul but didn't smell like anything rotten. More like something very old and musty, like moldy sheetrock. The women stepped inside the darkened room, sliding their hands along the walls inside the door hunting for a light switch. Mikayla reached up and pulled a thin chain hanging from the ceiling, illuminating the room.

THE SMALL HOURS

Jay couldn't believe what he was seeing. The room was nothing more than an old garage. The flooring had been ripped out, and if there had been a concrete slab, it was long gone now. Several mounds of dirt, each about three feet tall, surrounded a giant pit in the ground. Shovels and post-diggers were stacked against the wall. The pit was the oblong shape of a casket, but much larger than a grave, unless it was meant for several bodies.

But whose?

The stench made Jay's eyes water. Jesus Christ, what the fuck had they stumbled upon?

Willi tugged Jay's shoulder, pointing over at the far-left corner of the room. There, next to a shovel with a broken handle, was a pile of clothes. Old jeans, bras, shoes, dress shirts, all piled up like a load ready for the laundry.

Or ready to be burned?

Monica sauntered to the other side of the pit, careful to avoid walking through clumps of dirt in her heels. She looked down into the pit and then at the other two girls. "All is well," she said.

Quinten stepped over a large pile of dirt and moved closer to the edge of the hole. He looked down, his eyes wide. "What the fuck is that?"

Mikayla and Flo approached the side of the pit. A large pulley was suspended from the ceiling, reinforced with metal rods that ran the length of the room. A chain ran through the pulley, one side coiled on the ground next to the pit, the other end descending into the hole. Flo picked the chain up from the ground while Mikayla steadied the line.

"Pull him up, girls," Monica said, beaming.

The chain clacked through the pulley, the sound loud enough to grate Jay's nerves. Whatever was in the pit would soon be at the surface.

Quinten stepped back and joined the others. "We've got to get the fuck out of here, right now," he said quietly.

"You're not going anywhere," Monica said, wagging her

finger at them. "Speak as quietly as you please, whisper if you want. But trust me, I can hear you."

Arty rocked back and forth on his heels. He looked like he was ready to faint.

A large platform emerged from the hole in the ground. It appeared to be part of a hurricane fence, like a large gate.

Jay could not wrap his mind around what it was he was looking at.

It looked like a pile of dusty old clothes.

No.

There were two shapes, one much smaller than the other. Jay realized the smaller pile wasn't clothes at all, but a canvas sack. Mikayla grabbed the platform and began to pull it to her so she could slide it onto the ground next to the crater. Moving the small canvas sack off the platform, she turned to the pile of clothes. She unfolded the fabric, grains of dirt falling through the links of the platform.

Mikayla was prying open a folded, mummified body.

She started above the legs, bending arms long rigid with dry rot. The corpse looked so old Jay was surprised it was still in one piece.

Well, two pieces.

The body on the platform didn't have a head, or at least none that Jay could see.

"What's in the bag?" he asked.

"Wouldn't you like to know?" Mikayla said, her eyes fixed on the body.

Fields was a killer. Jay was right all along. Jay quickly took out his phone, opening the camera app.

Quinten looked annoyed. "What part of 'don't bring your phone' did you not understand?" He balled his fists. "I told you . . . I thought you left it back at my house."

Jay held up the phone, snapping pictures of the pile of clothes, the tools, and the pit. "We're way past that point. Let them track me, a little breaking and entering is nothing compared to this shit."

"Hey," Monica said, wagging her long-nailed finger at him, "what happened to our little deal?"

Jay snapped the shutter. "You said you wanted to see what was in here. Fields is a rat, at least according to you. These pictures are going to bring him down."

The women looked at each other, then started laughing.

"This one wants to be the hero," Flo said.

"He doesn't have it in him," Monica said, quickly walking around the pit to stand in front of Jay. "Give me your phone."

"No."

Monica's face changed. She was mad, no doubt, but it was more than anger. Jay could have sworn her eyes were lighter earlier, a hazel grey color, but now they were positively black. A low growl rattled from her throat. She bared a mouth full of fangs.

Not only the incisors.

Every tooth.

"Give me the fucking phone," she said, her voice now a loud hiss.

Jay slid his phone into his pants pocket. "No way."

Monica hissed at him again, lashing an arm out to grab at Jay. He backed away, barely evading her grasp. She swiped at him again.

Quinten stepped up behind her with a shovel in hand. As Mikayla and Flo screamed, he swung the blade down on Monica's head. The sound the shovel made against her skull was solid but wet, a sickening crunch Jay was sure he'd never forget. Monica's neck was bent at an awkward angle, her head no longer aligned with her shoulders and spine. Quinten swung again, missing her head and hitting her neck. The edge of the shovel cut deep into her flesh. Purple tinted blood spurted from the wound, splattering her shoulders and chest. Monica fell to her knees, swayed for a moment, then collapsed next to the pit.

Flo pointed a finger and hissed at Quinten, revealing

her own mouthful of fangs. Mikayla kept her attention on the platform. She opened the canvas sack and removed a petrified head. "Help me," she yelled at Flo. Hesitating, Flo rushed over to Mikayla's side and pulled the dried-up corpse closer.

It looked like they were trying to put the head back on the body.

What in the hell was going on?

Willi pulled at Jay's hand. He tore his eyes away from the women. Willi was screaming at him, but he couldn't decipher what she was saying.

All he could hear was the sound of that shovel hitting Monica's head.

CHAPTER TWELVE

"**S**NAP OUT OF IT," Willi shrieked. There was no telling how long she'd been screaming at him. Spit and tears spewed as she yelled in his face, and he couldn't hear a word of it.

Jay shook his head, his hearing rushing back. Quinten and Arty were at his side now as well. "Dude, we've got to go. Now!" Arty said.

Jay nodded. He wondered if he was in shock. If he was, he didn't like it.

He never wanted to feel like this again.

"C'mon," Willi yelled, "Out, out, *OUT!*"

He took in her tearstained face. Seeing her cry made him want to cry.

He glanced back at the carnage behind him. Blood continued to gush from the wound in Monica's neck. Quinten had damn near cut her head off with the shovel. That was self-defense, right? Surely the police would see it that way.

Ancient dead bodies retrieved from a meticulously excavated abyss, piles of clothing everywhere, the pulley system. This carnage had been going on for a long, long time. Jay didn't want to chance looking in the hole, afraid of what else he might see there.

The two women were now lifting the corpse off the platform.

Were they trying to make that rotting corpse stand up?

Arty pushed Jay to the front of the shed, but Jay couldn't take his eyes off the women.

Flo held the body under the arms. With the torso balanced on her chest, she grabbed the decapitated head from Mikayla and held it in place on top of the neck.

Mikayla pushed the sleeve of her leather jacket up, exposing her forearm.

"Hurry," Flo said, either oblivious to everyone standing there or simply ignoring them. Mikayla used her teeth to rip into the flesh of her wrist. Dark blood erupted from the wound. Flo used one hand to pry open the corpse's mouth, the other still holding it against the stump of the neck.

They were going to feed the corpse her blood.

Mikayla raised her arm and let the blood spill from her wrist into the open mouth of the corpse.

Quinten still held the shovel, his chest heaving with deep breaths. Arty kept pushing Jay closer to the entrance of the shed, his sneakers slipping in the blood on the ground.

Willi finally quit yelling. She faced Flo and Mikayla. "What the fuck?"

Jay couldn't make out any of the corpse's facial features. Clumps of dirt clung to straggly hair, the unkempt beard matted with Mikayla's blood. The man's body was dressed in an old long-sleeved shirt and trousers, both stained rusty brown. The shirt was buttoned down the front, and there was a ragged hole near the heart. Fields must have stabbed the guy, then cut off his head. This might have been his first kill. Jay had heard about serial killers keeping trophies of their victims, an ear here, a finger there, but a whole body?

This had gone from 'take some pictures of a t-shirt and send them to the police' right into Ed Gein territory.

Jay couldn't tear his eyes away from the scene in front of him.

The entire room had descended into chaos.

This is Hell, Jay thought, this is Hell and we're all going to die.

Flo slowly loosened her grip on the man's head, and when she let go, it miraculously stayed put on his neck.

THE SMALL HOURS

How was that even possible?

"Rise," Mikayla said, locking eyes with Flo. "Rise."

"Rise," Flo said, chanting with Mikayla now.

A clump of dirt, run through with dead grass roots, fell away from the top of the man's face, exposing a sunken socket. His lid opened wide, and a bloodshot eye stared out.

Jay felt a scream in his throat, felt it build and build inside, but he couldn't let it out.

Willi backed away, whimpering.

"It's moving," Arty said, pointing at the body.

Mikayla pulled her arm away from the man's mouth. The dead man's legs shifted, feet sliding on the ground, searching for purchase.

"Holy fucking shit," Quinten said. Jay turned to him and saw that his friend had gone completely pale.

No, no no, not now, dammit. "Quinten," Jay croaked.

The man's feet stopped sliding on the ground. Mikayla and Flo relaxed their hold on the body and allowed him to stand on its own. The dead man swayed for a second, almost losing balance, arms flailing wildly. He regained his footing, wavered for a second, then stood, completely motionless except for that left eye. The body was no longer simply a skeleton in dirty clothes. The flesh of his arms, legs, and torso filled out, and he was made whole again.

Alive.

He looked all around the room. A shaky hand cleared mud from his other eye so it could open.

The man wasn't breathing. Breath wasn't something Jay normally noticed while looking at someone, but in this case, it was disturbingly obvious. The man's chest wasn't moving at all.

The dead man's eyes roamed the room before focusing on Mikayla and Flo, who stood at the ready by his side.

A look of anguish tore through the man's features when he noticed Monica's broken body slumped near the pit. A guttural howl rushed through his lips, raspy at first, but growing in pitch and volume until Jay's ears were ringing.

Whoever this guy was, he was fucking pissed.

Jay then realized two things: his friends had vanished, and the women were both completely naked.

What the fuck?

Flo was standing right in front of him. He hadn't even noticed her moving. Jay looked over her body. He couldn't help himself. She reached out and placed a hand on his chest, slowly moving it down his stomach, lingering near the button on his pants.

Jay felt himself grow hard.

Flo's nipples tightened. "Yes," she said. Mikayla appeared behind Flo and wrapped her arms around her shoulders, caressing her. "Don't you want to fuck us?" Mikayla asked. Their faces were back to normal now. No, better than normal.

Jay had never seen anyone so beautiful.

Beyond them, the pit was gone. In its place was a large bed with red satin sheets. Soft music was playing, a song he thought he knew but couldn't place, and the air smelled of cinnamon. Flo gripped Jay's hand, gently tugging him toward the bed.

Jay stood his ground. "This isn't right."

Flo smiled, her lips wet, teeth gleaming. "Oh . . . it's right. It's so good."

"So good," Mikayla added, her voice a purr.

"Come fuck us." Flo tugged his hand a little harder.

Jay felt his feet moving without his permission. When he looked down, he could still see the dirt floor. The pit was gone, with a luxurious bed in its place, but the floor was still the same as before. Reality was trying to break through, but when the fantasy was this good, he almost didn't care.

He took a step.

"Come on, Jay, fuck us," Mikayla said.

Flo grabbed his crotch with her other hand, fondling

his erection through his pants. "You are ready. Can't you smell me? I'm so wet."

Jay could smell her. An inviting, musky scent. And something else, faintly creeping through the cinnamon.

The odor of rot.

Decay.

He took another step then found himself unable to move any further. He could tell that something significant was happening behind him, but he couldn't bring himself to care. Out of sight, out of mind.

Flo stepped up and wrapped her arms around him, her face so close to Jay's.

Her mouth so close to his mouth.

Their lips almost touching.

Yet something was pulling him back. Something urgent. A loud roar split his eardrums.

Flo's lips brushed against his, and then Mikayla was there too, her pink tongue flickering near Flo's mouth. She kissed Flo, sucked her tongue for a few seconds, and then kissed Jay.

They both kissed him.

Flo's hands roamed over him, touching and prodding.

Pleading.

Begging.

His penis was out now, Flo's cool fingers rubbing the head against her pubic mound. She was so slick, he could enter her right there. Stand there and fuck her with Mikayla helping, cradling his balls with her soft fingers.

The rush in his ears was louder now. Something was moving behind him, just out of sight. He could see movement in the corner of his eye. A hand reached out from behind him, clenching his shoulder. Fingers dug into his flesh and pulled him back.

Just a few more seconds.

A breeze rippled over the sheets on the bed, calling to him. For the briefest second, a shadowy glimpse of a fantasy grew in his mind's eye. Willi lay naked on the bed, writhing in ecstasy, beckoning Jay to join her.

To join them.

The hand on his shoulder pulled again, hard. Jay blinked slowly and when he opened his eyes, the bed was gone.

Flo and Mikayla were still very naked.

And they were very hungry. Their black tongues flickered over the fangs that lined their mouths.

Jay looked down. He was inches away from the edge of the pit. He could see down to the bottom, could see a long metal spike buried deep in the earth, its tip glistening with blood and viscera. Below the spike, scraps of torn flesh and bones littered the dirt floor.

The hands pulling him back were Willi and Arty, doing their best to keep him from falling to his death.

They tugged at him again, gripping his shirt tight, yanking him back. The vision in his head drifted away like a mist, and all Jay could see now was Flo's true face, her eyes inky black, mouth open, fangs at his throat. As Arty and Willi pulled him back, Flo's jaws clamped shut, her teeth grazing his neck. Jay lost his balance and fell backward, coming to his senses and scooting as far away from the pit as he could. He quickly grabbed at his throat, expecting to feel blood gushing from where Flo bit him, but there was only a scrape. He rubbed specks of blood from his palm onto his pants.

The dead man roared again. He knelt beside Monica's lifeless body and cradled her in his arms, muttering to himself. "No . . . no . . . no . . . " He raised his head and glared at the women.

Mikayla and Flo pointed at Quinten. "The tall one," they said.

The man stood and moved quickly to where Quinten was standing. He was fast, but Quinten was prepared, thrusting the shovel at the man. "C'mon fuckface, show me what you got."

The man screamed.

"You don't say," Quinten said, prodding the man with the end of the shovel.

THE SMALL HOURS

The man grabbed the shovel and pulled it away from Quinten, tossing it aside. He then reached for Quinten, who barely dodged his grasp. The man lunged again, this time gripping Quinten's shirt with one dirty hand. He lifted Quinten off his feet and shook him violently. Arty came up behind the man, who merely swatted him away like he was a rag doll.

Quinten kicked the man square in the crotch. It was a hard kick, one that would have brought any normal man down, but clearly this man wasn't normal at all, because the blow didn't even phase him. The man leaned forward, his mouth opened wide. Rows of long, sharp fangs dug into Quinten's neck. The sound Quinten made started as a scream, but was reduced to a choking gurgle as the fangs tore his throat open. The wound was large and ragged. The man pulled the flesh from Quinten's neck away in one swift motion and spit it onto the ground. Blood jetted from Quinten's severed arteries, and the man leaned forward to capture the blood in his mouth. He bit Quinten again, deeper this time, digging into the muscles of his neck, tearing so much tissue away that Quinten's head flopped back, no longer able to support itself.

They watched as the man, who had been dead mere minutes before, drank from the fountain of blood erupting from Quinten's neck.

Willi screamed. It was a guttural sound that pierced Jay's eardrums. Jay pulled her closer to him, backing away.

The man bit Quinten again, this time nearly severing his head. Quinten's head rolled against his back, a single stretched-out strap of flesh keeping it attached to his ravaged neck. The drinking continued. Mikayla and Flo stood next to the man, basking in the blood misting from Quinten's neck. Blood splattered their naked skin as they cupped their hands to catch the spray.

The man, sated, flung Quinten's body away. He sniffed the air, nostrils flaring. The group was unable to move as the man's eyes roamed over each of them. Jay felt his gorge rising in his throat as the man appraised him. Moving faster than humanly possible, the dead man shoved his way through the room and out the door.

He was gone.

CHAPTER THIRTEEN

ARTY PUSHED HIMSELF to his feet, nearly stumbling into the pit. The women continued feeding on the blood from Quinten's body, lapping at the precious blood before it soaked into the dirt. Arty picked up an old hoe that was leaning against the wall near a pile of clothes and paused. He grabbed a t-shirt and held it up. "This is her shirt, right?"

Jay nodded. It was LuCyndi's shirt, no doubt about it.

"Holy shit," Willi said.

Arty wadded the t-shirt into a ball and tossed it to Willi.

"I was right about Fields," Jay said. "I was right, and you were too." He looked over at Willi, tears streaming down his cheeks. "You were right to be worried. This . . . this . . . " he waved his arms around, "this is all my fault. All my fucking fault."

Willi grabbed Jay's hand.

Jay couldn't say anything. There wasn't anything to say. He knew now he should have listened to Willi. He should have gone to the police. Now his friend was dead, and his killer had walked past them as though nothing happened.

LuCyndi's killer too.

They were out of their league, way over their heads in a world of shit, and it was his fault.

Arty poked the handle of the hoe at the women still crouched around Quinten's body. "Get back," he yelled.

Mikayla stood and wiped blood from her mouth with the back of her arm. Arty thrust the wooden end of the hoe at her chest, catching her right under her right collarbone. "I said get. The. Fuck. Back."

Using the wooden handle, he pushed Mikayla and Flo back from Quinten's body. Arty then knelt next to his fallen friend and started digging in Quinten's pockets. He found a set of keys, but no wallet or I.D. He loosened Quinten's belt and pulled it through the loops of his pants.

Jay couldn't believe Arty was going through Quinten's stuff. "What the fuck are you doing?"

Arty held up Quinten's knife. It wasn't as large as a Bowie knife, but it looked sharp enough and would probably work in a pinch. "We're going to need this." When Arty held up the blade in the belt scabbard, both Flo and Mikayla backed away from it, hissing.

"Ah, silver," Jay said.

"Uh, no. It's stainless steel. He got it from the knife show we went to last year at the civic center."

"Then why are they reacting to it?" Willi asked.

Arty shrugged. "Don't like knives, I guess." Arty held it high, pointing the scabbard at the women. They cowered, whimpering in fear.

"Let's go. Time to go to the police," Willi said.

They turned to leave. The room reminded Jay of a torture pit he'd seen in some old B-Horror flick, except this time Vincent Price wasn't slinking around the pit, laughing with madness. There was no telling how many people Fields had lured back here. All those bones in the pit. So many dead. He still wasn't sure what he had witnessed, almost refused to believe it had happened at all. And the way those women had affected him, the visions they'd put in his head. They had somehow slowed time down. What felt like an eternity in the hallucination was really a few seconds. They had tricked him, trying to get him to step into the pit. No matter how he fell, that metal rod would have impaled him, likely killing him.

The police were going to have a field day searching the shed.

THE SMALL HOURS

It was a crime scene.

They were standing in a crime scene.

And Quinten was dead.

Jay knew Quinten's mother was dead, and that it had hit his dad real hard. Quinten too, though he didn't admit it. But you could tell. Sometimes Quinten would get quiet when someone mentioned their own mother. Grief was a motherfucker. Quinten's father had certainly had his fair share of it already, and now his son was gone.

Oh dear Lord.

Jay took Willi's hand, and alongside Arty, they walked to the door. Willi reached the door first, but it swung open before her fingers could grab the knob.

A shadow passed across the doorway.

For a split second, Jay thought the dead man had come back for them.

To finish the job.

A figure stepped into the light.

It was Fields, back early from his trip. He stood in the doorway with a handgun and a smile on his face.

"Welcome to Fright Night. For real." Fields laughed at his little joke. He waved the pistol, motioning for them to step back into the shed. "Ha, I've been waiting so long to say that."

"How . . . "

"How? You know, the cellphone is a wonderful creation. Amazing how it interacts with security systems."

Jay nodded. So there *had* been cameras, but they had missed them somehow. They walked backward, away from Fields, inching closer to the torture room.

"I see those bitches used my fucking keys," Fields said. This time he was not laughing. "You know, you just can't trust the help these days. You give someone a chance to do something, to make a better life, and they squander it away like it's nothing. And you," he said, pointing the gun at Jay, "so many opportunities to not fuck things up, and you turn out to be the biggest fuck up of all. So much potential. Your whole life ahead of you, a beautiful girlfriend, and poof, now it's all gone."

Jay thought fast. "We came here to get a head start on the gutters. It got dark so we were putting some tools away, and that's when the girls showed up."

Fields nodded. "I know, I know."

"They went crazy, tore the place up. They . . . they . . . "

Fields smiled. "Yes, yes, terrible tragedy. So sad."

"You believe me, right?"

A shot rang out as Fields fired into the ceiling of the shed. "Of course not. Remember my phone? I watched you and your friends break into my shed. So please, save all the lies, the pleading, all of the bullshit." He aimed the gun at them, forcing them back into the torture pit room. He walked past them, taking in the mayhem. Stepping over Monica's body, Fields stopped and examined what was left of Quinten. Mikayla and Flo were huddled in the corner, clutching their clothes, shielding their nakedness from Fields. He shook his head at them. "You fucking bitches. What the fuck were you thinking? Can you tell me that, without lying?"

They wailed and cowered under his gaze.

Fields turned back to Jay, Willie, and Arty. "Okay. Real simple question. Requires a simple answer."

Jay gulped.

Fields raised his arm and aimed the gun at them. "Where's my fucking vampire?"

CHAPTER FOURTEEN

JAY DIDN'T KNOW what to say. His mind refused to register that word—vampire—though that was, unquestionably, what he had witnessed. It was a vampire that had killed Quinten. The women were vampires as well. And somehow Fields held control over them all.

"Well? Where?" Fields walked around Quinten's body and stood in front of Willi, placing the gun against her forehead. Fresh tears sprung from Willie's eyes.

"I don't . . . I don't know. He left," Willi stammered.

"No." Fields pressed the barrel of the gun harder into Willi's forehead. "You don't talk. This question is for Jay, he will decide your fate." Fields kept his eyes on Willi. "Where did he go?"

"I don't know," Jay said.

"That's not good enough." Fields pulled the pistol's hammer back. "I cleaned this gun yesterday. It may look old, but it's in excellent working condition. It has never misfired. At this range, the back of her head will be splattered all over that wall unless you tell me where he went."

"You're asking me a question I don't know the answer to. He's your vampire, wouldn't you know?"

Jay watched Fields' finger tense around the trigger.

"Oh, I do know where he's not . . . he's not here. You set him free," Fields said.

"Wrong answer. The women set him free. They pulled

him out of that pit, and . . . I don't know . . . put his head back on, then he killed Quinten, then he left. He looked like he was in a hurry."

Fields turned to Jay. "Don't get cocky with me." For a second, the gun left Willi's forehead. Her eyes were squeezed shut. Jay could feel her trembling.

Willi's eyes snapped open. She knocked Fields' arm down and quickly snatched the gun away from him. Thankfully, it didn't go off. Fields glanced at his empty hand in surprise. Willi aimed the gun at him, motioned for him to get back.

"You fucking bitch," Fields said. He kept looking at his hand as though he could blame it for losing the gun.

Willi aimed the gun at Fields' face. Jay didn't even know she could handle a gun, let alone take one away from someone. "Get back," she said. Her grip on the gun was steady.

Holding up his hands, Fields slowly stepped back. "Okay. Okay. I'm stepping back." He walked backward, carefully avoiding the hole in the ground. "Maybe this is just a misunderstanding. Right? How are you to know where he went?"

Fields lunged at Willi, reaching for the gun. She lowered it and fired. The sound was nothing more than a POP, not as loud as Jay expected. Blood erupted from Fields' kneecap. He fell to the ground, screaming in agony. "Goddammit. Fucking bitch shot me."

Flo was creeping along the side of the pit, making her way toward them. Arty pulled the knife from the scabbard and held it up and Flo fled back into the corner with Mikayla. For some reason, they were more afraid of the knife than the gun.

Writhing in pain, Fields flopped and rolled on the ground. He grabbed his knee, howling in agony when his hands touched the wound. Willi aimed the gun at his head. "Get up," she said.

"Get up? Are you serious? Goddamned sexual chocolate telling me to get up with my kneecap blown off."

THE SMALL HOURS

Jay grabbed one of the shovels near the side of the pit. The handle was broken off, but the end looked sturdy enough. He slammed the shovel down on Fields' head, knocking him out.

Jay and Willi grabbed Fields by his legs and pulled him out of the room. Arty stood guard by the door, and once they were clear of the room, he held up the keys, jingling them at Flo and Mikayla. "Good night, ladies."

The women growled at him and Flo gave him the finger.

Arty locked the metal door behind him and then helped Jay and Willi drag Fields out of the shed.

Jay let go of Fields' legs and wiped his hands on his pants. "Where to?"

"Inside," Willi said, looking at the house.

"Shouldn't we take him to the police?"

Willi bit her lip. "Not yet."

"You sure about that?" Arty said. "The longer we wait, the worse this gets."

"There's nothing we can do to bring Quinten back. He reacted in self-defense, and those women . . . they're not normal. This motherfucker is still alive, and once the police have him, he's going to lawyer up and we will never know the truth."

"Are you sure you still want to know the truth?" Jay asked. He wasn't so sure himself. He knew that sometimes exposing all the lies and secrets only made things more painful. And Fields had a lot of secrets.

Willi looked down at Fields. "Yes. I need to know. LuCyndi would have done the same for me." She looked up at Jay. "Is your phone charged?"

"Enough."

"Good. We're going to record this fucker's confession."

CHAPTER FIFTEEN

IT TOOK ALL three of them to lift Fields onto the recliner in the living room. Jay pushed the lever on the side of the chair to kick out the footrest. Fields groaned when his leg extended but remained unconscious. There was no telling how long he would be out, and they didn't need to take any chances on him waking up and getting away. Jay figured Fields wouldn't get too far with his knee fucked up, but people can surprise you sometimes, and the last thing they needed was another surprise.

Jay was tired of surprises.

They broke into the shed, got the evidence, so far so good. Everything was downhill from that point on.

No more surprises.

Jay started pulling drawers open in the kitchen, looking for duct tape. Electrical tape would work, if there was enough of it. He found a drawer full of cigarette lighters. Hundreds of them, all colors and sizes. Were these from Fields' victims? Another drawer contained towels, another silverware. There wasn't any tape.

What the hell, who doesn't have tape?

"You find anything?" Willi yelled. She was in the living room with Arty, searching through the cabinets of Fields' entertainment center.

Jay joined them in the living room. "Nothing."

Arty snapped his fingers. "Wires."

Willi's eyes grew wide. "Electrical wires? *YES* . . . the

lamps . . . unplug the lamps, anything that plugs into the wall. We can use the cords to tie him up."

Arty and Willi went around the living room unplugging the lamps. They ripped the cords out from the base of the lamps and used them to secure Fields' legs to the footrest of the recliner.

"Make 'em tight, these cords stretch," Willi said.

"What about his hands?" Jay asked. With all the lamps unplugged, the room was especially dark, and now the only light was from the ceiling fan overhead, which they didn't want to turn on in case the neighbors had heard any of the commotion from earlier. They were lucky the police weren't busting down the door already. Jay assumed they were on their way, no need to draw attention to themselves in the meantime. Jay worked through a quick statement in his head in the event the police did show up. He imagined the worst: a SWAT team rappelling through the windows, snipers on the rooftops of the house across the street, local news vans encircling the house, Eye-in-the-Sky helicopter at the ready for the inevitable high-speed chase. "*We* knew *he was the killer, and we had to take matters into our own hands. We* did *tell you about him, several times.* You *didn't want to listen. Justice for LuCyndi. Justice for Quinten. Fields is a serial killer.*"

Only Fields wasn't exactly a serial killer, was he?

No, there was something else going on, and Jay didn't have an explanation for it.

"Tie two cords together for his hands," Arty said, showing Jay how the socket ends could be looped together to make a longer cord. One of the lamp cords was quite stubborn, refusing to come loose from the base of the lamp. Willi looped it around Fields' neck and stretched the cord to plug it back into the wall socket.

"Don't strangle him," Jay said.

When they'd finished tying Fields to the recliner, they all stood back and took a breather.

"Vampires," Willi said.

"Fucking vampires. It's . . . unbelievable," Jay said.

Arty nodded. "But we all saw it. I mean, y'all saw what I saw."

"They were doing something to our minds. I felt it." Willi hugged herself and shivered. "It was like a finger was poking around in my head."

"They were hypnotizing us. When you pulled me back, I didn't even know how close I was to the pit. All I saw was what they wanted me to see."

"What did you see?" Willi asked.

Jay shook his head violently. "They put . . . images . . . sexual images . . . in my head. And they're still bouncing around inside."

"And they did something with time," Arty added, "one second the women were clothed, the next . . . naked. Weird."

"I never saw them move. They were all over me like that," Jay snapped his fingers for effect.

Willi looked at them wide-eyed. "The lady in white. At the park . . . you think it was them?"

Jay nodded slowly. "Could be. Probably."

Willi clamped her hand over her mouth.

"What?"

She started pacing, shaking her hands while she walked. "Oh shit, oh shit, oh shit."

"What? C'mon, tell us."

"You think Luce could be a vampire?"

Jay grabbed Willi's shoulders and pulled her to him. "I don't think it works that way."

"Then how does it work? What if Luce is the one who killed Timothy?"

"She would have made herself known to you," Arty said. "If that part of the legend is true, then the rest of it has to be true. Has Luce been coming to you at night while you sleep?"

"No."

"They always hurt the ones that love them the most, and she's never come back to me."

THE SMALL HOURS

"I think that's more a part of werewolf folklore than vampires," Jay said.

Willi pulled away from Jay. "Fuck this shit." She walked over to the recliner, twisted the switch on the lamp near Fields' head, and aimed the light directly at his face. "Interrogation time."

Jay opened the voice recorder app on his phone. Fields remained unmoving in the recliner, oblivious to the bright light shining in his face. "He's not waking up."

Willi looked around the room and made her way to the bar. She grabbed a bottle of Grey Goose and pulled the cork out. "This'll wake his ass up." She splashed vodka on Fields' busted kneecap.

Fields only winced, then groaned in pain.

Willi poured another shot, and this time Fields' eyes popped open.

"What the fuck?" Fields shook his head, grimacing.

"Surprise motherfucker." Willi said.

Fields struggled against the cords binding him to the recliner. Unable to get free, he leaned his head back and huffed out a giggle. "Fine, fine. Tie me up. The Master will return."

"You wanted to kill me earlier when you were so desperate to know where he went, now all of the sudden he's coming back?"

Fields shrugged. "Doesn't matter."

"Who is that man?" Jay palmed his neck to see if the scrape was still bleeding. His hand came back dry.

"No. Not man. Master."

"Looked like a man to me," Willi said.

"And yet you saw what he did to your friend. He will return. Your annihilation is imminent."

Willi held the bottle over Fields' kneecap. "If you're so sure, then where did he go?"

Fields looked at the bottle. "A terrible waste of my vodka, but please, pour all you want. The nerves in my knee have grown accustomed to the sting.

Jay moved the lamp closer to Fields' eyes, tightening the cord. "When will he come back?"

Fields giggled. The sound was annoying, like a car engine struggling to turn over because the battery was nearly dead. "Soon. He must have left to find his bride. Quinten ended the other one, so now it's time for her replacement to come home."

"How do you know his name?" Jay asked.

"Who, Quinten? My dear boy, who do you think mowed my lawn before you came along?"

Willi glanced over to Jay. "He's so full of shit. Everything that comes out of his mouth is a lie." She splashed vodka in Fields' face. "Nothing but a slimy bullshit artist."

Jay shoved the lamp at Fields. "Fucking liar."

Willi leaned close to Fields. "And you said 'bride'? What do you mean, bride?"

Fields rolled his eyes. "The women? Those hoochie mommas are his brides."

"Hoochie mommas?"

"Strippers. They're strippers. Well, they used to be strippers. Exotic dancers. At the clubs."

She was getting tired of Fields. "And they were vampires as well."

Fields nodded. "Crazy huh? I see one of them got you." Fields nodded at Jay, eyeing his throat.

"Just a scrape."

Willi looked at him with alarm.

Jay tried to laugh it off. "I'm fine."

"Doesn't matter, the end is near. Now either kill me or let me rest until he returns." Fields shut his eyes.

Willi poured more vodka on his kneecap. He was right, the liquid fire was no longer affecting him. Fields didn't even flinch. "Arrogant bastard," she said. "Did this Master kill Timothy Rice too?"

Fields' eyes flew open and he shook his head violently. "No. Absolutely not. The Master wouldn't do that."

THE SMALL HOURS

"But the Master did kill LuCyndi?"

"I don't know if the Master killed anyone. You have no proof of it."

Willi smiled. "Oh, we've got proof."

Fields smiled back, then closed his eyes again.

Willi turned the lamp off and let it hang over the back of the recliner. Jay slumped on the sofa and kicked his feet up on the coffee table. Under normal circumstances, he would have never done something so rude, but he couldn't find it within himself to bother being respectful.

Arty paced the living room nervously.

Willi sat next to Jay and examined the scrape on his neck. "Looks bad."

Jay shrugged. "It's not. I'm fine."

"Promise to tell me if that changes."

"Of course."

Arty stopped pacing. "Is anyone else hungry?"

Willi shook her head. Fields kept his eyes closed but raised his hand as far as the cords would let him. "There's food in the fridge. I believe there are some oysters leftover from our little snack the other day," Fields said.

Jay was starving. He couldn't believe that he was hungry after everything that had happened, but the rumble in his gut told him otherwise. Unfortunately, oysters were the last thing he wanted to eat.

Arty looked at Fields. "Raw oysters?"

Fields nodded.

"You like to eat oysters?" Willi asked, wrinkling her nose.

Arty smiled. "Fucking love 'em."

"You know they're alive until you eat them, right?" Jay said, sharing the tidbit of information he'd learned from Fields.

Fields smiled. "That's my boy."

"Fuck you."

Arty went into the kitchen to raid the icebox.

"There's ham and cheese in there too," Fields said. He

opened his eyes and rolled his head in a circle like he was cracking his neck. "And a steak. Raw. Wouldn't you like a raw, bloody steak right now, Jay? Doesn't that sound . . . perfect?"

"Why would I want a raw steak?"

Fields grinned at him. "You will. Soon."

Arty came back from the kitchen with a plate of ham and cheese and a large Ziplock bag of oysters in their shells. He slid a chair into the space between the recliner and the sofa and sat down, grabbing slices of ham and cheese and rolling them up.

Jay and Willi stared at him, Willi's mouth hanging open.

"What?" Arty said between bites. "Told y'all I was hungry."

"How can you eat right now?" Willi asked.

"Dr. Jo calls it stress eating. I eat and eat, then worry about things so much my metabolism kicks in high gear. Then I get depressed. Guess that's why I'm in treatment. Eventually, all this eating is going to catch up with me."

Fields waved his strapped-down hand as high as he could. "I'm in treatment. Dr. Syward is good."

"Whatever she's doing for you isn't working, considering everything you've done," Willi said.

"Exactly what have I done?"

Willi held up her hand and began counting on her fingers. "Well, let's see . . . kidnapping, murder, hiding evidence . . . "

Fields scoffed. "Who have I kidnapped? Who did I kill?"

"My girlfriend," Arty said. He had the Ziplock bag open and was trying to use a butter knife to get into one of the oysters.

"I have done no such thing. You have broken into my home, killed a woman, and released the Master, who in turn killed your friend, obviously in self-defense. I wasn't even here. When I did arrive, after my surveillance system notified me of a break-in, you shot me in the knee."

"Bullshit," Willi said, her voice rising. She picked up LuCyndi's t-shirt from where she'd lain it on the arm of the sofa. "How do you explain this?"

Fields shrugged. "That's your proof? Obviously, that's nothing to do with me."

"It was in your shed."

"The Master might have brought it here, how do I know? Maybe there's more to all of this than you think? Suppose even half of what you claim is true, then maybe I know things you don't know. What if I'm not at liberty to say? Perhaps I was keeping the rest of you safe?"

Jay laughed. "Seriously. No wonder you're in therapy."

"I wonder how the police will look at it. Have you thought about that? How do you know I haven't been in contact with the authorities already? How do you know I haven't told them about this alleged killer that took up residence in my work shed without my knowledge? How do you know I'm not an operative working to bring an internationally wanted criminal to justice?"

"Wouldn't the police know about it?" Willi asked.

"Suppose I'm deep undercover? What if they know but are unable to say anything? See, these are things you haven't thought of. I seriously doubt you've looked at every single conceivable angle. You think I'm a killer, but now you know that you're going to have to come up with some outlandish story to cover your asses."

Willi laughed at him. "You're crazy. And a killer."

"No. Not a killer. You have no proof. Only a giant pile of bullshit made worse because you didn't think it through."

Willi looked at Jay. "Don't listen to him, obviously he'll say anything at this point."

Jay nodded. "He's involved, no doubt. An accessory to murder, at the very least."

Fields shook his head violently. "Bullshit." He looked over at Arty, who was still trying to open the oyster. "And you are in no danger of getting into that shell."

Arty took a deep breath and shoved the butter knife against the oyster shell again. "I'll get it."

Fields nodded back to the kitchen. "In the drawer next to the sink, there's a short double-sided blade with a white handle. Fetch it and I'll tell you how to open it."

Arty kept trying to pop the shell with a look of dogged determination on his face. After several moments, he gave up, tossing the shell on the plate.

"The knife? Get it please," Fields said.

Arty huffed and went into the kitchen. When he returned, he showed the knife to Fields. "This knife?"

"Yes son, you've done well. Now pick up the oyster and place the edge of the blade at the thick end. Gently press until you feel it slide in and twist the blade until the shell pops."

Arty did as instructed but didn't have much luck. The oyster shell was damp with condensation, and he couldn't get a good grip on it. The blade was sharp enough, it just wouldn't slip into the shell. He started to grab a different oyster from the bag, but Fields stopped him.

"There's nothing wrong with that oyster you have now. Relax and try again. I couldn't open the shell the first time I tried either. Jay knows how to do it, maybe he could assist."

Jay held up his hands. "I'm out. Can't even think about food right now, especially fucking oysters."

"Are you thinking of the story you're going to tell the police?" Fields smiled, obviously enjoying himself. "The police will find out, of course. They always do. I'm willing to bet one of the neighbors noticed all the commotion going on here and called them. They could be on their way right now. They could be outside, waiting for the right moment to bust down the doors. *On the ground motherfuckers! YOU MOVE, YOU DIE!*" He laughed. "I can't wait to see the look on your faces."

Jay stood and walked into the kitchen. He wasn't thirsty, but he started opening cabinets until he found the glasses. He ran the tap and drank lukewarm water. Fields was right, they were fucked, and it was all his fault. He didn't know what to do. Going to the police was out of the question. Suppose Fields was some kind of undercover operative? What if he had this whole thing wrong? He refilled the glass and drank again.

The man in the shed had killed Quinten, but that wouldn't have happened if he would have only listened to Willi. He couldn't change the fact that Quinten had killed one of the women, but that was kind of self-defense, right? The last time Jay had checked, people did have the right to defend themselves. But what if the police didn't see it that way?

What if the police were in on it?

What if they had accidentally ruined an entire investigation because they put their noses where they didn't belong?

Willi joined him in the kitchen. He handed her the glass and she finished off the water. "We're fucked," Jay said.

She shook her head.

"It's all my fault."

"Bullshit," she said.

"Bullshit? Quinten's dead. We let that man escape. He was the killer. Maybe Fields was holding him for the authorities to come and get him. He's probably some crazy serial killer from Europe and we let him go."

"Um . . . you saw them put his head back on, right? That wasn't a man."

"He was 'the Master,'" Jay said with air quotes. He gave Willi a weak smile. "I don't know what I saw."

"We all saw it. Things are weird and maybe we should have called the police, but we didn't and now we're here and we're this close to justice."

"You think so?"

"Yes. Quinten killed that woman in self-defense, the man . . . or whatever . . . retaliated. Fields is involved. He's feeding us a line of bullshit because we're letting him, but he's part of it. Me, you, and Arty, the *only* thing we've done is break into his shed."

"You shot him."

"Self-defense."

"So now what?"

Willi shrugged. "I don't know. Part of me wants to call the police and let the chips fall where they fall. At least it'll be over and people who do this shit for living will be able to take over. But I kind of want to get Fields to admit to something. Anything. We get him on a recording, and he's done."

"He's not going to talk."

Willi smiled. "We just haven't tried hard enough." She set the glass down on the counter and wrapped her arms around Jay. "Something tells me everything is going to work out."

Jay squeezed her back, inhaling the scent of her skin.

Willi stepped back. "You okay?"

Jay nodded, checking the scratch on his neck. "Yeah. Feeling fine actually."

"You're cold."

Jay rubbed his hands together. "Might need to turn the heater on."

Fields began to laugh from the living room. Jay and Willi walked over to where he was tied to the recliner. Fields was giggling, furiously trying to cut through his bindings with the white-handled knife. Arty lay on the floor next to Fields. Jay opened his mouth to yell at Arty to get up, but the words died on his lips when he heard Willi's sharp intake of breath.

Arty wasn't moving.

The wound in Arty's throat wasn't very big, was really nothing more than a puncture mark, and it didn't seem large enough for all the blood that was gushing out of Arty's neck. The pool of blood was growing larger by the second, seeping through the cracks in the tile, inching to the rug under the recliner and coffee table. Jay grabbed the knife from Fields and held it to his right eye.

Still giggling, Fields lifted his head slowly, very aware of the blade less than an inch from his eye. "Ooops. Now, I've actually killed someone."

CHAPTER SIXTEEN

JAY KEPT THE knife on Fields while Willi flipped Arty over and checked for a pulse, pulling her hands away from his bloody throat in despair. "Fuck, fuck, fuck."

"What?"

She looked at Jay, tears in her eyes. "He's dead."

"Dead?"

She looked back at Arty. "I don't know CPR, but I think we're well past that anyway."

"We've got to do something."

Willi knelt on the floor, Arty's blood staining her knees. "He's not breathing." She grabbed his wrist. "No pulse."

Fields laughed at them. "Look, I shucked an oyster."

"Motherfucker," Jay said, jabbing the knife into Fields' cheek.

"Do it," Fields said, leering. A thin dribble of blood rolled down the side of his face. "Explain *that* to the police. Go on, do it."

Jay pulled the knife back and kicked the side of the recliner. Fields winced in pain from the jolt. "Just shut the fuck up," Jay said, thrusting the knife at Fields again.

Willi pressed on Arty's chest like she'd see in a thousand movies. Jay wasn't sure if she was doing it right but deep down inside he knew it didn't matter anyway.

"Call the police," Fields said.

Jay pulled his phone out of his pocket. "I'll do it, motherfucker."

"*Call them now.*"

THE SMALL HOURS

Willi stood and pulled the gun from the waistband of her pants. She leaned over Fields and put the barrel against his forehead. Fields giggled at her.

"Put the phone away," she told Jay.

Jay looked at her. He was thinking maybe it *was* time to call the police. Let the experts take over. "You sure?"

She pressed the gun harder against Fields' head. "Do you think all of this will have a positive outcome when the police show up and I'm the one holding the gun? In Texas?"

She had a point. Jay put his phone back in his pocket. Willi had a look in her eyes he hadn't seen before. A look that said she meant business.

"Call the cops," Fields hissed.

"No. No more fucking around. You're going to tell us everything, or I'm going to fuck you up," Willi said.

Fields rolled his eyes. "Please. Give me a break. Fuck me up? I'd laugh if it wasn't so pathetic."

Willi lowered the gun to his blown-out kneecap. "You know, I could shoot it again. You're already going to need a cane if you make it out of this, so I might as well really fuck it up. Maybe there's a wheelchair in your future." She shifted the gun to his other knee. "Or . . . or, I could take this one out too. From this range, I doubt you'd have much left. The bullet would blow a hole straight through your leg at this range. Hell, by the time we did call the police, you'd have lost so much blood that whatever's left of the leg would be seriously damaged. Hate for an infection to set in. Then you'd definitely need a wheelchair. Kinda hard to hobble around on two messed up legs."

Fields nodded. "Sure thing, sugar."

"Sugar?"

Fields smiled. "Yeah, whatever . . . sugar. Bitch. Whore. Whichever you prefer. How many bullets do you have left? Do you even know how to check? Of course, it doesn't matter anyway, when the Master returns, you're all dead. Your friend on the floor over there will make a nice little appetizer. Then he will feast."

"Who is the Master?" Willi asked.

"The Master? A monster, now. At one time he was an aristocrat. Do you know what that word means, or does the Texas public school system suck as bad as they say?"

"I know what aristocrat means."

"He was rich. A one percenter. A ladies' man, the world at his feet. But he dabbled around with some shit he should have left alone and fucked up his whole life. It corrupted him."

"So he's been a vampire the whole time," Jay said.

Fields smirked. "Ha . . . funny. He got bored, decided to live in America. He paid a hefty price getting here. But he had . . . urges. Urges that were easy to exploit. He nearly killed my whole crew, but we caught him . . . and tamed him."

"He works for you?" Jay asked.

"Well, he did, but now he's out. He's under the spell of the night. And you killed one of his brides. He's gone rogue. Beyond my control."

"Yet you say he's *your* Master?"

"He is."

Jay was getting tired of these little games. "But he works for you?"

"Is it wrong to admire the monster you brought into the world? Did not the good doctor Frankenstein admire his creation?"

Now it was Willi's turn to smile. "At first, until his creation revealed who the true monster was. Learned that shit in eleventh-grade literature."

"Good! There's hope for you yet."

"Where do we find him?"

Fields shrugged. "Who knows. No need to look for him though, he'll be back."

"What makes you so sure? For all we know, he's gone for good."

Fields shook his head. "He will return before sunrise. That much I know for certain. And then you will all die."

"Not if we're gone," Jay said.

Fields looked at Jay. "Run if you want. Far, far away. But he's got your scent, and if he doesn't kill you tonight, he'll hunt you down. Once he's had a taste of you, there's no escape." His eyes glanced over to Jay. "You'll know soon enough."

Jay felt the scratch on his neck. The wound was crusted over, didn't even hurt anymore. Fields was fucking with him, he felt fine. He turned his head, swiveled it around on his neck. Not even sore.

Willi kept the gun aimed at Fields and continued to press him. "Turn on the recorder on your phone," she said to Jay.

Once the recording started, Willi asked Fields the question that had brought them here in the first place. "Who killed LuCyndi?"

"Not me," Fields said.

"The Master?"

He nodded.

"Say it."

Fields started to laugh, but stopped abruptly. Willi started to say something, but Jay cut her off. "Shhhhh, listen."

Nobody spoke.

Jay glanced at the back door. The porch light wasn't on, and the entire backyard was completely dark, but he could see that there was someone standing at the back door. Through the blinds on the door, he could only see a human-shaped shadow, but there was no doubt about it . . . someone was out there. Jay slowly raised his hand and pointed. Willi turned, aiming the gun at the door.

The doorknob jiggled.

Whoever was outside was trying to get in.

The knob jiggled again, and then began turning. Jay's breath caught in his throat. The door opened slowly. A dark figure stepped into the house, their pale hand reaching for the light switch on the wall. When they flipped the switch, the ceiling fan above them began to turn, but the lights did not come on.

Jay grabbed the lamp hanging from the back of the recliner and turned the light on, aiming it at the figure in the door.

A tall man wearing a black hoodie stood there, carrying a large leather duffle bag. He was clearly shocked to see that he wasn't alone. He held up his free hand when he saw the gun Willi was holding. "Whoa," the man said, "could you please not point that at me?"

"Who the fuck are you?" Willi asked, keeping the gun aimed at him.

Jay knew that voice. "Erick?"

The man's eyes went to Jay. "Hey man, what's going on here?"

"I was about to ask you the same question," Jay said.

"You know him?" Willi asked, sneaking a glance at Jay behind her.

"Yeah. It's Erick the Red."

Willi shook her head, confused.

"My weed dealer."

"Ohhh," Willi said.

Erick slowly lowered his hood, revealing his face. "I asked first. Why are you here, and why is Renny tied to that recliner?"

"Erick," Fields said, "Thank God you're here. They broke into my house. The girl is crazy . . . she shot me in the leg."

Erick looked at the bloody mess of Fields' leg. "Damn."

"Renny?" Jay asked. "Who the fuck is Renny?"

"I am," Fields said.

"Is that name even Russian?" Jay asked.

"My name could be Rumpelstiltskin, doesn't fucking matter. What matters is Erick is here. My savior, thank God."

Erick met Fields' eyes. "I'm not your savior."

"Then *why* are you here?" Willi asked.

"I've come to kill the beast, but it looks like I might be a little late to the party."

Jay and Willi looked at each other. "Wait, you know what's been going on?"

Erick nodded. "You two need to leave, now. You've got no business here. Forget everything you've seen."

Willi shook her head. "Little too late for that shit. This *beast* you mentioned killed my best friend and Quinten, and *Renny's* crazy ass friends almost killed us. And Fields killed Arty himself. We ain't going nowhere."

Erick's shoulders slumped. "Goddamn it."

"I asked you about Fields the other night," Jay said, anger rising in his voice. "You knew about this shit, and you didn't say anything?"

"What could I say? I didn't know what you knew, especially since you were being so vague. No way was I going to give myself up. I've been working on this for a long time. A real long time."

"Are you even a drug dealer?"

Erick nodded. "It's a front, but yeah, I'm legit."

"Who do you work for?" Willi asked.

"People," Erick said.

"Like a company?"

"Well, it's not like we have a logo and business cards and shit. Definitely don't have annual sales meetings in Hawaii to celebrate who killed the most vampires for the quarter."

"You motherfucker," Fields said, spittle spraying from his mouth. "All this time, you've been watching me like a bitch?"

Erick nodded. "You were too easy."

"Too easy. I'm an expert at this. That's why I'm doing this job, no one else could ever manage the Master."

A gentle smile spread across Erick's lips. "You have certain flaws."

"Nonsense."

"The Master is controlling you. And the beast is loose

and out and about for a night on the town. So much for managing. Of course, you can't see it, you're too close. You worship the beast, you're infatuated with him."

Fields scowled at Erick but managed to maintain eye contact. Erick was making him squirm. "You are the one who is infatuated. Following me around. I should have realized . . . Erick Von Holson. Ha, someone did some creative spelling at Ellis Island . . . am I right? How in the world you ever zeroed in on me, Lord knows, but the fact that you've got it all wrong only confirms your ineptitude."

"Sure, whatever you say. Care to explain to the class why you've been letting the beast roam free?"

Fields looked down at his hands.

"C'mon . . . we're waiting."

"He . . . escaped. I turned my back for one second and he got out. I used him to eliminate enemies, that much is true. He is quite efficient, very little mess or fuss. But he got the best of me. I'm not perfect. Only human."

"He got the best of you three times?"

Fields shook his head and clamped his mouth shut.

Erick leaned in closer to Fields. "What you got? Nothing? That's what I figured."

Jay cleared his throat. "What now?"

Erick unzipped the duffle bag that he'd dropped on the floor. He pulled out a set of poles that had threads at the ends and began to connect them, twisting each pole as tight as he could. "This ends tonight," he said. There was now one pole, nearly eight feet long. He attached a point to one end, then turned the handle at the other end, releasing a set of hooks from within at the end of the pole. The hooks were designed to open after the sharp point pierced through the flesh. "The beast will return before the sun rises. If it has fed, then its only focus will be getting back into the dirt. If the beast hasn't fed, that would be a good thing, but it would make my job more difficult."

"Why?"

"Because he'll be desperate. There's nothing worse

than a hungry vampire, especially right before the sun rises. Getting into its sacred soil is paramount, but the need to feed is strongest at that time as well. I also don't want him to feed because if he's drank fresh blood, he'll be stronger. Either way, it's going to be a bitch."

Fields giggled. "Facing the beast during the small hours has been a fatal mistake for many hunters."

Erick turned the pole around and thrust the pointed end at Fields' face, stopping a few centimeters from his nose. "That's why you're the bait."

PART THREE:

THE SMALL HOURS

CHAPTER SEVENTEEN

JAY WENT BACK into the kitchen to get another drink of water. He filled the glass from the tap, feeling his stomach churn in revolt. Something wasn't right, and his paranoia wasn't helping one bit. He took a few sips, struggling to swallow.

Jay wasn't sure if he could feel his pulse or not. Making sure no one was watching, he felt his wrist.

He'd known something was wrong earlier when he was talking to Erick in the living room, but he didn't want to make a big production out of it. It was a feeling of nausea and dizziness. More than likely he was hungry, but his nerves were wrecked. Who could eat at a time like this?

Jay suddenly realized he hadn't been breathing.

Panicked, he gasped, drawing a ragged breath. So, he still could breathe. Maybe he had been holding his breath? Jay did that sometimes when he had a lot on his mind or was trying to do something more mental than menial. Air still flowed in and out of his lungs, as long as he thought about it.

Breathing was something hardwired into every living thing in the world, something we took for granted until it became strictly voluntary.

And there was no doubt his breathing was voluntary.

No, not voluntary.

Optional.

He felt his wrist again, then the crook of his elbow.

Placing a hand on his chest, Jay's fears were confirmed.

He didn't have a pulse.

At some point while talking to Erick in the living room, Jay had casually passed away. Apparently, the scratch on his neck was something he should have been very worried about. That's all it took, a simple scrape on his neck. Not a bite, an abrasion. Didn't even hurt. Barely even bled.

A graze from the incisor of a vampire.

Enough to turn him.

Beyond the expected *freaking the fuck out*, Jay didn't know what to do. Now wasn't the best time to announce his situation, especially with a vampire hunter in the house.

If he said anything, would the slayer turn on him?

If he didn't say anything, would it make things worse later?

Telling Willi probably wasn't a good idea either. She was good at keeping secrets, but there was no way she'd be able to keep quiet about something of this magnitude.

Despite all of this, Jay felt weird about dying. Like, he was seriously worried how Willi would handle the news.

Hint: *Not well.*

But in the grand scheme of things, it wasn't that big of a deal.

Everyone dies, right?

Knowing he was dead and would remember everything that came after?

Who in the hell ever got to do that?

Vampires, that's who.

Yeah, this was probably the part of him that was turning into a vampire somehow keeping him calm about the whole thing. Jay had wondered earlier whether, if he did start turning, it would be something he could resist, fight away with all his might. But no, it was all very simple . . . first you're dead, annnnnd . . . now you're a vampire.

No way to fight it, just accept it and move on.

Except moving on meant embracing it, and that probably wasn't such a hot idea at the time.

THE SMALL HOURS

Jay opened the refrigerator and stared at the contents. He went through waves of feeling like he was starving, then feeling like he was about to vomit. Everything in the fridge looked so unappealing. A Tupperware container caught his attention. Inside were boiled shrimp tails, still in the shell. The smell coming off the shrimp was overpowering. Was that another one of his new powers, the sharpening of his senses? He put the container back on the shelf.

Could he even eat regular food?

The jury was out on that, going by all the movies he'd seen. Vampires in film were very inconsistent, some could eat food, others became violently ill. If he ate something and got sick, the others would probably think it was just nerves.

But what if they didn't? What if Erick thought it was something very different than frayed nerves?

Jay figured what he needed was a joint.

Fuck. Could he even get high now?

A raw steak wrapped in butcher's paper sat on the bottom shelf, just as Fields promised earlier.

Jay picked up the package. The label said it was a ribeye, but that didn't matter. He could smell the meat. It was so strong, so pungent. Earlier, Fields mentioned something about the blood from the steak, but Jay knew better than that. Unless you killed the cow yourself, the chances of getting a "bloody" steak from your local butcher were slim to none. Myoglobin, not blood, gives raw meat its color, only Fields was too dumb to know that tidbit of mostly useless information.

Jay's mouth began to water.

It wasn't blood.

It was the meat. The raw meat.

He put the steak back on the shelf and stared at his shaking hands.

Footsteps approached from behind. He stood and shut the fridge. When he turned around, Willi was stepping into the kitchen—he'd heard her walking over the living room carpet as though she was already right behind him. She frowned when she saw his face. "You okay?"

Jay shook his head. "I . . . this is all so much." His hands wouldn't stop shaking. He rubbed them over his face, hoping Willi wouldn't notice.

She grabbed his hands to steady them. "You're flushed."

"I feel like I'm freezing."

"Well, lurking in front of the open refrigerator door isn't helping."

"No doubt."

"Hungry?"

"I'm good."

Willi nodded over at Erick in the living room. "Erick seems like he knows what he's doing."

Jay was hoping Erick wasn't all that great at his job, actually. "Yeah, I guess. I mean . . . what kind of training is there for vampire hunters? Is that like an online course? What are the prerequisites for that program? Experience using a hammer? Wielding a crucifix?"

Willi rolled her eyes. "He has a plan. You trust him, right?"

"He's not who he says he is, but it does explain how he walked out of the police department with his weed, if that story is meant to be believed."

"What?"

"Nothing. Just a story. I hope he doesn't make things worse."

They went back into the living room. Erick had untied Fields and had his hands in cuffs behind his back.

"Where'd you get the handcuffs?" Jay asked.

"Always come prepared." Erick's gaze lingered on Jay a little too long. "Hey man, this is all going to work out, okay?"

"I know."

"You look a little worried."

"Scared."

"That too. Don't worry, my plan's going to work. We need to get Fields back into the shed."

"Yes, please take me back to exactly where I want to be," Fields said, gloating. "The Master comes, the trap is set."

"Shut up," they all said in unison.

Jay cleared his throat. "Once we get in the shed . . . "

Erick slung his bag over his shoulder. "We wait. Then we kill it."

CHAPTER EIGHTEEN

ERICK SHUT THE door to the shed behind them while Jay and Willi led the way into the back area. Willi unlocked the door, then stood back so Erick could open it. He looked back at her before pulling the door open. "That boy on the floor back in the house?"

She nodded. "Arty Holemwood, LuCyndi's boyfriend."

"Damn, this has turned into a shitshow."

"He's not going to . . . you know? Come back?"

Erick shook his head. "Not unless he was bitten. Or scratched. Usually, it's a bite, something in the saliva, but I've heard a scratch can get you too."

Jay listened to them, forcing himself not to touch his neck. Maybe Erick hadn't seen the scratch yet. Maybe Erick thought it was a wound from struggling with Fields earlier.

"You ready?"

They nodded.

Erick stared at them. "Okay, so crosses don't work, and sunlight only makes them slightly weaker. There are only two things they care about . . . their sacred dirt, and blood. As it gets closer to dawn, the dirt becomes the most important. They must return to their soil to survive, and without blood, they lose their supernatural abilities. Everything they do, everything they make you see in your mind, it's a facade. They're nothing more than rotting meat sacks. You're going to see them as they really are, because the closer we get to dawn, the weaker their hallucinogenic powers are. They're dead. Just keep telling yourself that. They're dead." Erick pulled the door open.

Jay was sure someone was standing behind the door, waiting for them. He wanted to warn Erick, to tell him not to open the door, but he knew if he did, Erick would wonder how Jay knew something, and that was the last thing Jay needed.

The room was dark. The foul stench of blood and shit and rotting flesh permeated the air.

Something moved in the darkness, coming towards them.

Willi put her hand over her mouth to stifle her scream and stepped back, while Erick held his metal rod steady in front of him.

Quinten stepped into the doorway, a shit-eating grin plastered across his face. "What's up, assholes?" His voice was ragged, like he'd gargled with Drano and broken glass. Quinten said something else, but Jay couldn't make it out over Willi's cries.

When Jay last saw Quinten, he was a crumpled mass on the ground, his head nearly severed by the beast. Now, Quinten, like Jay, was undead and very aware of the situation. Congealed blood stained the area around the wound in Quinten's neck. The right side of Quinten's face was stretched ghoulishly from the broken shovel handle he jammed through his eye socket and cheek, down into his shoulder and chest to keep his head on straight. His right eye bulged out from the pressure of the handle and continued to make erratic movements, as though unable to keep focus.

And, to top it all off, Quinten was naked.

With an erection.

Erick stood back, keeping his spear close to Quinten. "Friend of yours?"

Jay nodded. "The Master killed him."

Erick nodded and thrust his spear into Quinten's chest. Though he was undead, Quinten was still fast on his feet and tried to dodge away from the spear. It missed his heart but connected with his shoulder. Quinten laughed at Erick. "C'mon slick, you gotta do better than that."

Erick pulled the spear out and lunged again.

Quinten held up his hands. "Dude, what is your deal?"

"*Stay the fuck back!*" Erick yelled.

Jay grabbed Erick by the shoulder. "Hold on a sec," he said, pushing himself in front of Erick. "Quin, dude . . . you know something's not right, yeah?"

Quinten nodded, the movement restricted by the wooden handle. "Yep. You still have all your clothes on. Shit is fucked, man. C'mon, get naked. You too, Willi, and uh . . . whatever your name is."

"Quinten, you're dead. That man, he killed you."

Quinten stared at Jay then laughed. "No shit, Sherlock. You're not looking so good yourself."

Jay ignored him. "We're still your friends, you know that."

"Yep. We're all friends here in the funhouse. That doesn't change anything."

"It changes everything."

Quinten cracked a blood-smeared grin. "I'm still going to eat you. All of you."

"And that's why I'm going to take you down," Erick said, thrusting the metal pole past Jay, striking Quinten in the chest. The sharpened end pierced Quinten's heart and burst through his back, spraying blood behind him. Erick twisted the handle, releasing the metal hooks at the end, and pulled on the pole, sinking the hooks into Quinten's back. Screeching in pain, Quinten reached out for Erick, swiping with hands that now looked more like claws, sharp talons grazing the air, but never making contact with Erick. Erick pushed Quinten backward, guiding him to the left of the pit. On the other side of the room, Flo and Mikayla wailed in agony, their true forms revealed at last.

It was now clear that both women had been dead for a long, long time. They weren't pretty anymore. Time and decay had ravaged the flesh of their faces, eyes and cheeks sunken, lips black, and in Flo's case, missing altogether. Wisps of hair, stringy and matted with blood, hung from their bony scalps. Broken fangs, uneven and crooked but more dangerous than ever, lined their mouths, while their tongues, black and swollen with oozing sores, flickered out rapidly, as though tasting the air, forever hunting for blood.

Erick looked over his shoulder at Jay. "Quick," he yelled, "grab that shovel."

Jay stood frozen, wondering how things had gotten so out of hand so fast. Never in his wildest nightmares would he have believed Quinten could have survived what the vampire did to him, but there he was. Although, said a quiet voice, *Quinten is a vampire now. He didn't survive at all.* Even though Quinten was a vampire, maybe a part of him could still be normal, could still be one of them, a friend.

Erick hadn't even given him a chance. Was this what was in store for Jay once Erick realized he was a vampire too?

"C'mon Jay, get the damn shovel." Erick was struggling to hold Quinten. Even with the hooks pierced through his body, Quinten was giving Erick one hell of a fight.

Jay walked over to where the shovel lay on the ground. He looked back at Willi, who was crying, her face twisted ugly and raw, and he promised himself he never wanted to see her face look like that again.

Fields stood behind Willi, smiling, as though killing Quinten all over again was a win. In a way, it was. Killing Quinten was both a win and a loss. Jay picked up the shovel and walked over to where Erick had Quinten pinned to the ground. The stench of rotting flesh burned his nostrils, but it wasn't unpleasant.

It kind of smelled good.

Jay grimaced and forced a retching sound through his throat. Anything to keep Erick from suspecting the worst.

"Hit him in the neck. Don't worry about that handle jammed in through his face. Aim for the neck."

Jay held the shovel above Quinten's body. His friend looked back at him, legs flailing in the dirt, trying to get a grip on the blood-soaked, muddy floor while Erick held him down with the metal rod.

Don't make eye contact.

Too late.

Jay locked eyes with Quinten. They stared at each other, tears welling up in Quinten's good eye, the other eye bulging from the socket.

"Do it," Erick said.

Jay couldn't take his eyes off Quinten. His friend stopped crying as a sly smile spread across his face, along with a look of realization.

"He won't do it," Quinten said.

"*Do it! Hit him!*" Erick pressed the metal rod down hard, pinning Quinten to the dirt and clay below.

Jay let the shovel drop to the ground. "I . . . I can't."

"Can't, or won't?"

Jay couldn't say anything.

Quinten started laughing. "My brother. Now in more ways than one."

Quinten knew. He knew what Jay was now and was willing to spill the beans to save himself. Jay couldn't tell if Erick was listening to Quinten or ignoring him.

"Here," Erick said, passing the rod to Jay, "hold him down and I'll do it."

"Let me up," Quinten said, his teeth smeared with blood. "Jay, you can do this. Help me . . . help your brother, we're the—"

Quinten's words were cut off as the shovel struck his neck, severing his windpipe. Gouts of thick black blood oozed from the wound. Erick lifted the shovel and slammed it down again, harder this time. He hit Quinten again, and again, breaking the wooden handle that was shoved through his neck and face. Jay held Quinten down while Erick finished the job, Quinten's legs twisting in death throes. When he was done, Quinten's head was completely separated from his body. Erick scooped it up with the shovel and tossed it into the pit beside them. Jay lifted the rod, trying to pick up Quinten's body. He could feel the power in his hands and arms, power he had never possessed before. Jay could have lifted Quinten off the ground with one hand, but there was no way he was going to let Erick see that.

Jay let Quinten lay on the ground. "I can't lift him."

Erick dropped the shovel and took the rod from Jay. He lifted Quinten effortlessly, the hooks on the end of the rod holding the lifeless body aloft until it was over the pit. Erick twisted the handle to release the hooks, sending a shower of blood over the yawning gap onto Willi and Fields as Quinten's body fell into the pit.

Jay stood next to Erick. He was covered in blood. It soaked his face and hair, dripping near his mouth. Quinten's nasty black blood, but blood nonetheless. The urge to lick it off his lips was maddening. The precious fluid was so close, yet he forced himself with all of the will in his body and soul to stop himself from licking it up. Quinten had almost given him up, and now Jay was determined not to do the same.

Erick wiped the blood off the end of the metal rod with an old rag he found on the ground. "I know that was hard," he said, not looking at Jay.

Jay nodded and looked over at Erick. He did his best not to change his expression. "He was my friend."

"And your brother."

"No, just a friend."

Erick's mouth narrowed. "Do you trust me?"

Jay shrugged. "Sure."

"You're going to have to trust me if you want out of this, okay? I don't have all the answers, but I know a few things. I need you to trust me."

"Okay."

"Say it."

"I trust you."

Erick rolled his eyes. "Once more with feeling."

Jay sighed, making an effort so Erick could see him inhaling and exhaling. "I trust you."

Erick looked over at Willi. "You trust me?"

Fields leaned forward. "It's a trick," he said to Willi like she was his secret confidant.

Willi nodded. "I trust you."

Erick smiled, but it wasn't a happy smile. It was grim and determined. "Good." He lifted the rod, aiming it directly at Jay.

Jay backed up. "What the fuck, man?"

"Hey . . . hey . . . it's going to be okay. Trust me, remember? Move over there." Erick nodded to where Mikayla and Flo were sitting near the rear door of the shed.

"What the hell, Erick?" Willi screamed.

Jay stood his ground. "What has gotten into you, man?"

Erick thrust the rod at Jay. "Don't think I won't do it."

"I'm not moving."

The cold end of the rod rested against Jay's chest, right above his heart. He could feel the tip pressing through his shirt. He could hear a pounding, deep and strong, like someone was beating on the side of the shed.

It was Erick's heartbeat.

He could hear and feel Erick's heart as though it was in his hands, pressed close to his ear.

"When's the last time you took a breath?" Erick pressed the rod against his chest a little harder.

"*Jaaaaaaayyyyy!*" Willi's scream was raw and piercing. Jay winced, the pain physical and sickening.

Jay forced himself to breathe.

"You get an A for effort," Erick said, "Hell, I'll even give you a gold star next to that A, but right now you *have* to trust me. If you care about Willi, you'll do as I say."

Jay looked over at Willi. She knew. He could tell. She

knew what he was now, and there was nothing he could do about it.

Jay grabbed the rod with both hands, moved it away from his chest effortlessly even as Erick tried to hold it steady. "Put it down."

"You going to move?"

Jay let go of the metal rod and walked over to Mikayla and Flo. They wailed as he got near, but didn't attack him. Their cries weren't cries of fear, but of welcome. He was one of them now. He looked at Willi, mouthing the words "I'm sorry."

She mouthed back, "I love you."

Fields was laughing through all of it. "Ha, the bitches got him. That tiny scratch did a number on you, Jay. Now you'll know the power. It's glorious, so glorious. Embrace it, bask in it, let it flow through your veins. The Master comes, and only through him can you survive."

Willi spun around and punched Fields in the nose. His eyes crossed for a second before rolling back into his head. Fields collapsed before he could make another sound. Willi looked back at Erick. "You want us to trust you? Get us out of this shit."

CHAPTER NINETEEN

"**DO YOU EVEN** have a plan?" Jay asked. He sat on the ground, leaning against the rear door of the shed.

Erick lay the metal rod on the ground and went to his duffle bag. "As a matter of fact, I do." He took out two cloth bags, each fastened at the top with a thin string. He tossed them over to Jay. "Put them near the door."

Jay picked up the bags. "What are these?"

"I can't say in mixed company."

Jay pushed himself off the wall to do as Erick asked. Flo slithered over to Jay and got in his face. Her breath reeked but the smell didn't bother Jay at all. The odor was strong, but it was welcoming to him, like the smell of warm bread fresh out of the oven. She touched his face, grazed her cold fingers over his lips. Jay watched as a piece of rotting skin hanging from her forearm broke off and fell on his shirt. He brushed it away, but not before he saw it wiggling, as though still alive. That had to be a trick of his mind, right? He pushed her away, surprised how light her body was, like moving a sack of bones. She crawled over to where Mikayla was lying on the ground and wrapped her bony arms around her as though to keep her warm.

"What are you going to do to Jay?" Willi asked. Her voice was wrecked from crying. She pushed her sweaty hair back away from her face.

"Nothing. As long as he doesn't feed, he'll be fine after we kill the beast."

"Fine? As in normal? As in alive?"

Erick's smile was grim but confident. "Trust me."

"You keep saying that, yet you've shoved my boyfriend over there in the corner with the other two vampires like you're prepping them for the firing squad."

"I'm saving your fucking life, okay? Jay is not in control right now. The closer he is to you, the easier it will be for him to give in to his new urges."

"Afraid he's going to hypnotize me or something?"

"No. He can't do that, not until after he feeds and sleeps in his dirt."

"Like a ritual?"

Erick shrugged. "It's how they survive. There's not much magic to it. Everyone thinks of spells and ancient books with arcane rites that conjure demons. That's all bullshit. To do that kind of magic, you have to prepare, for weeks, months, sometimes years. Everything must be exactly perfect and even then, shit doesn't always work right. About twenty-five percent of the time, it might work, and honestly, the odds are probably even less than that. Sometimes you get to see your dead aunt one last time, sometimes you resurrect a frog halfway across the world. There's nothing magical about this . . . blood and dirt. That's it."

"Wow, thanks for the lesson," Jay said.

"And thank you for attending my TED talk." Erick wiped his hair away from his face and twisted it into a quick ponytail. "Serious talk now, time's getting away from us. We've only got a little time before dawn. He'll be back before then, and we don't know what kind of shape he'll be in. If he's fed, we're probably fucked. Hopefully he hasn't, which will make him a little weaker, easier to put down."

"Fields didn't have a problem keeping him down here," Willi said, pointing into the pit.

"This is true, but Fields also kept him supplied with fresh bodies. There's no telling how many people have died in this room. We're here to kill him, and he's going to know that as soon as he gets into the shed, if he doesn't already. We move quickly and we take care of business."

"What do you want me to do?" Jay asked.

"Stay put."

"You don't trust me?"

"No. Sorry, but I'm sure your girlfriend will appreciate it."

Jay punched his fist into the dirt. "I'm just a worthless liability."

Erick cast Jay a grim look. "Not taking any chances." He glanced at his duffle bag and then back at Jay. "There is something you can do."

Jay perked up. "What?"

"See if you can open that door behind you."

Jay stood and turned the several deadbolts on the door and twisted the knob. The door opened.

"Good. Now put those sacks outside the door." He nodded over at Flo and Mikayla. "Make sure those two don't try to sneak out."

Jay picked up the sacks. "What are these for?"

"We might need them later. Once he gets inside, you'll need to open the door and light them. The cord will burn, and once the sacks begin to smolder, they'll turn blue. That will protect us."

"Magic?"

Erick shrugged. "Maybe. Could be an old superstition. The story goes that they'll keep him from getting out, and others from getting in."

"Others?"

"Yeah, if he's bitten anyone else, they'll come here to protect their master."

"There's more of them?"

"Yep, one of them is here right now."

Jay smirked at Erick. "Funny, asshole."

"I thought you said it took years for magic to work," Willi said, her voice dripping with sarcasm.

"Those bags *did* take years. Decades."

THE SMALL HOURS

"These two bags are going to protect us?" Jay asked. "What about the other door?"

"I've got more. You handle those, and I'll get the front entrance."

Doing as he was instructed, Jay opened the door and placed a bag on both sides of the entrance. With the door open, he could smell the world. Everything hit his nostrils at one time, the grass, the dirt, the trees, the air. A strange churning sound filled his ears. Was he hearing bugs and worms crawling through the grass, burrowing into the ground? The whole world was out there, all his for the taking. All he had to do was step outside. He could run, he knew he could get away. Didn't matter where he went, surely he could find somewhere they would never find him.

He shut the door and turned the deadbolts.

It would have been easy to run.

Too easy.

Willi deserved more than that.

Erick deserved more than that.

It wasn't anyone's fault but his own that he'd gotten scratched, and even then, he'd only been doing what he thought was right. All of this was to find LuCyndi's killer, and he'd done that. He'd been right all along, and now things were terrible in ways he could never have imagined, and yet . . . Erick seemed to have some hope for him.

Or he was bait.

Maybe a little of both.

Jay knew that if he showed an ounce of menace to either of them, he'd be dead meat.

It was getting harder and harder not to become a menace.

"You all right, babe?" Willi called out to him.

He nodded. Turning to see her standing on the other side of the pit, he knew he could never run. The very idea was just the beast inside him, trying to trick him.

And if he knew it would be trying trick him, he could keep it tampered down and maybe everything could work out.

CHAPTER TWENTY

ERICK KEPT LOOKING at his phone.

"Waiting on a call?" Willi asked.

"No . . . checking the time."

"It's still dark outside," Jay said.

"And that's when it's the most dangerous."

Willi laughed. "That 'darkest before the dawn' shit?"

"It's true. The night is darkest right before the sun rises. The small hours. Dangerous time. It's when the monsters come."

"How long have you been doing this?" Jay asked.

Erick reached into his pocket, took out a pack of cigarettes, and fished around inside until he pulled out a joint.

"What the hell, man?" Willi said.

"Yeah, what the hell. Fire it up," Jay said.

Erick lit the joint and took a hit. "This shit can't touch you now," he said to Jay after blowing a bluish plume of smoke. He coughed and hit the joint again. "And this is how I deal with shit, okay? No judging."

"Whatever. Fine, don't share."

"Seriously man, you won't get high. Only blood works for you. As long as you don't drink any, you've got a chance."

"Wait," Willi said, "shouldn't he kill the vampire who scratched him? That'll end it, right?"

"Depends." Erick walked over to where Monica's corpse lay on the ground. Time had not been kind to her.

THE SMALL HOURS

She was the oldest of the three women, and now that she was dead, it showed. She was nothing more than crumbling bones. "Is this the one that got you?"

Jay shook his head and pointed at Flo.

"Hmmm . . . I'm not sure."

"Then what makes you think he'll come out of this okay?" Willi asked.

Erick took a hit, held it for a moment. "We have to kill the source."

"And the Master is the source?"

"Exactly. Unless he transferred, but I'd have known about that already."

Willi's eyes narrowed. "Transferred?"

"Yeah. If he's wounded and knows he's not going to make it, he could have someone else out there, someone hidden away from here. If he knows there's not a chance, or if he has another bride out there, he'll make them the new Master."

"Like a hydra. Cut off one head, another grows in its place."

Erick nodded.

"He's the one who's been killing those kids, huh?" Willi asked.

Erick stared at the ground. "Probably."

"Will they turn?"

He shook his head. "They tend to leave the children out of their affairs."

"Other than killing them."

Erick pointed his finger at Willi and nodded. He put his joint out on his boot and dropped the roach into the cigarette pack. He stood and remained still for a few seconds, then picked up his metal pole from the ground.

"You hear something?" Jay asked.

"Did you?"

"No."

"Let's be quiet. Won't be long now."

Jay didn't know what time it was and didn't care. He

didn't want to know, because the closer it was to dawn, the sooner he was going to have to kill the beast, and he wanted to delay that as much as possible. He was scared. Or maybe he was really hungry. He leaned against the door and let himself slide down to sit on the floor. Flo stirred for a second, lifting her head before rolling off Mikayla. How long could they survive like that?

Was that his ultimate fate?

He kept thinking about what Willi said earlier, about LuCyndi being the woman in white. Maybe Luce killed Timothy Rice. But if that was so, why didn't she kill Carmen? Maybe Carmen had managed to get away from LuCyndi. She could have realized there was something wrong with her old babysitter. They could have struggled, and that might have been how Carmen got LuCyndi's hearing aid.

She could have remembered Carmen and decided not to kill her. But if that was true, then there was a possibility that LuCyndi was out there now. That would explain the vandalism at her gravesite. Maybe there wasn't any vandals at all, and Luce had dug herself out of her own grave. Clawed through the mud and pulled herself from the ground.

Willi would hate him for thinking about that.

Jay shook his head.

No, Luce was dead and buried, and she wasn't coming back.

Not now, not ever.

Mikayla sat up and looked over at Jay. She wasn't in as bad a shape as Flo, but still . . . it was gross. Her skin was covered in oozing sores, blood black as ink leaking all over her. Her blonde hair hung over her face, but Jay could see her eyes peeking through the greasy strands. Did she see him as some kind of kindred spirit, another member of her family?

Her blood brother?

The thought disgusted him.

Yet . . .

She moved quickly and shoved her face into his. Weakened or not, she was still fast. She pulled her hair away from her face, revealing a rotting hole in her cheek. He could see her tongue moving in her mouth, black and swollen.

"Not brother," she whispered, "Lover."

"Hey Jay," Erick said, holding his metal rod out in attack position, "you might want to take care of her. Like now."

"Kill her!" Willi yelled.

Jay brushed Mikayla away, but she only came back at him faster. Flo was starting to stand up. "Come to us, lover," Mikayla said, brushing her cracked and blistered lips against his ear. He could feel the cold, flaky skin.

It would be so easy to slip into her arms.

"Do something!" Erick screamed at him.

Flo was walking towards them. Jay grabbed Mikayla by the throat and held her away. He could feel the bones in her neck. He grabbed a handful of her hair and pulled hard. Clumps came off in his hand. He throttled her with both hands, bending her head back.

"Fucking kill her man!"

Mikayla looked up at Flo, who was standing above them. She smiled at her blood sister. Flo smiled back. "Do it," Mikayla said.

"With pleasure," Flo said. She then touched Mikayla's neck with her fingers, her nails digging into her flesh. Flo raked her nails across Mikayla's throat, slicing her skin open. Black blood spurted out. The blood turned to a stream and arced into Jay's face, into his mouth.

He backed away, trying to avoid the blood, but it was too late.

Willi screamed, but her voice sounded so far away.

So, so far away.

Jay couldn't help himself.

The blood filled his mouth. He knew he should spit it

out, but as black and nasty as it was, once he tasted it, he couldn't get enough. He swallowed the blood, gulped it down greedily. Erick was right there at his side, thrusting his weapon at Flo. The metal ripped through her rib cage. Jay watched as Erick twisted the handle, releasing the prongs. With the sharp metal hooks bursting through Flo's back, Erick tugged hard, and the rod exited the same way it went in, though this time, it made a much larger hole. The hooks tore a massive hole in Flo's torso. Chunks of rotting flesh fell on the ground next to Jay, and this time he was sure he saw it.

The flesh was moving.

Moving on its own, as though alive.

The undead, alive.

Jay pushed away from Erick, wondering if he was about to feel the hooks next.

"Dammit all to Hell," Erick said. He stepped up and kicked what remained of Flo into the pit, then used the metal rod to push Mikayla over the edge. Jay tried to stand, but Erick shoved the rod against his chest, pinning him down. Willi wailed on the other side of the pit, and now Jay could hear her, loud and clear.

"Goddamn it," Erick said.

"I'm . . . I couldn't help it."

Nodding, Erick lifted the end of the rod off Jay's chest. "They tricked you. I told you they were dangerous."

Jay wiped his mouth with the back of his arm. "Then why didn't you kill them earlier?"

"Why didn't you? You could have killed them easier than me. Hell, they would have never even suspected you of trying to harm them."

Jay licked his lips. He'd already swallowed the blood, so it probably didn't matter anymore. "I don't feel any different. Maybe it has to be someone else's blood, someone who's not a vampire."

Willi pointed at him. "Hmmm, babe . . . you might want to check your teeth."

Jay ran his tongue over his teeth. Mere seconds ago, they had been normal.

Now his teeth were gone.

His tongue grazed over the sharp spikes that now sat where his teeth used to be. "*What the fuck, man!*"

"Chill out," Erick said, "it was bound to happen anyway."

"You said I had to drink the blood to turn. I drank the blood, *I drank the fucking blood!*"

Erick held out his hand. "Stand up."

Jay grabbed his hand and allowed Erick to pull him up. Erick inspected the inside of Jay's mouth. "Little bitty baby fangs."

"Still fangs."

"Hey, calm down. Like I said, it was probably going to happen anyway."

Jay pushed Erick away. "Do you even know what the fuck you're doing?"

"Yes."

"' . . . *it was going to happen anyway* . . . ' What the hell does that mean?"

"You keep changing the rules," Willi said.

"No. No no no. I told y'all if he drank blood and slept in his dirt he'd be beyond hope. I'm *not* changing the rules." He turned to Jay. "Where were you born?"

"In Grigsby."

"Do you have a family plot, like in a cemetery?"

"What the fuck does that matter?"

"Do you?"

Jay didn't know. When he was a little boy his grandfather had died, and he remembered going to the cemetery across town. Years later, an aunt on the same side of the family had died, and she was buried at the memorial gardens right down the road. "I don't know . . . I don't think so."

"Has your family planned your funeral?"

"I don't think so. We don't focus on the morbid shit,

like dying. Nobody wakes up in the morning wondering where we'll all be buried. Who the hell does that?"

"Then you most likely don't have any dirt. There's a chance, a good one, that this will all end when we kill him."

"But you don't know that for sure," Willi said.

"Based on things I've seen, I know that when you kill the head vampire, the transformation will cease in those that haven't completely turned."

"But does that mean I'll be normal?" Jay asked. He grabbed Erick's arm. "Does that mean I'll be alive?"

"You should be. Probably. We can hope."

"You. Don't. Fucking. Know," Willi said.

Jay let go of Erick's arm. He motioned them to be quiet. "Shhhhh."

"What?"

Jay looked over at Willi. "He's coming."

"Are you sure?" Erick asked.

Jay nodded. "I can feel him."

CHAPTER TWENTY-ONE

WILLI WENT TO the wall and reached for the light switch.

"No, leave them on," Erick said, "he's coming in no matter what, and we need the light."

"Can't we keep him outside so the sun will make him weak?" she asked.

"The early morning sun won't be enough. He'd have to be exposed to it until noon for it to make a difference, and he's not going to wait that long. Get ready . . . grab something, he's going to go for whoever's closest."

Willi made her way to Quinten's duffle bag and started looking through his gear. She pulled out one of several knives stashed inside, then took the gun out of her waistband. "I've got this, and the gun."

"How many bullets?"

She shrugged. "I just know how to pull the trigger."

Erick scowled at her, then flashed a grim smile. "Doesn't matter. The knife will work better, the gun is going to only piss him off."

"I need to be near Willi," Jay said, starting to make his way around the side of the pit.

"No," Erick said, "stay there. He'll come to you. You're like one of his children now."

"I'm fucking bait," Jay said, throwing his hands up in the air.

The door behind Willi rattled. He was there. She moved to the canvas tarp that separated the front of the shed from the pit and pulled it shut to hide from the beast's view.

Jay kept running his tongue over his fangs. He could feel them growing longer in his mouth. His whole body tingled, and he could feel the man standing outside the shed more intensely now.

The Master.

He pushed the thought from his head. This man, this beast, wasn't his daddy, and Jay wasn't going to let it claim him as a son.

No way.

The canvas tarp lifted for a second, as though caught in a breeze, then ripped away. The man tossed the tarp aside and stepped into the pit room. He looked Erick over first, licking his lips, and then his gaze traveled to Willi. She had the gun raised, aiming at his head. The beast took a slow step in her direction. It was like he was toying with her, taking his time, fully confident how this was all going to end. Willi squeezed the trigger; the shot went wild and blasted a hole in the side of the shed. The beast advanced until he was close enough to grab her.

Willi aimed the gun directly at his face and squeezed the trigger.

The shot fired true. The bullet hit the beast directly in the face, ripping a hole in his cheek, exiting the back of his head. Blood and bits of skull and brain matter splattered into the air behind him.

The beast stopped in his tracks, rocked by the bullet. He reached up to touch his face, groaning in pain.

"It worked." She aimed again. "See, it hurt him."

The beast lowered his hands and roared at Willi, baring a mouthful of fangs.

"And he's pissed off," Erick said. He came up behind Willi, weapon raised, ready to attack. The beast glanced at him, and for a second Jay thought this was it, that the metal rod was going impale him and this would all be over. The beast swiped at Erick, knocking the pole from his grasp and flinging him into the air. Erick slammed into the lights hanging overhead, sparks and glass showering down from the busted bulbs. Jay watched as Erick seemed to hang in the air for a millisecond before falling to the ground.

"Get up!" Jay screamed.

The entire shed was dark now, but Jay could still see clearly.

He could see Erick lying motionless on the ground.

He screamed at Erick again. "C'mon man, get up!"

Jay couldn't tell if Erick was unconscious or dead.

Willi fired another wild shot at the beast and missed. He moved in fast, trying to knock the gun out of her hands. Willi tried to fire again but got nothing but an empty click. "Fuck!" She tossed the pistol aside and pulled out the knife.

The beast grabbed her by the throat and shook her violently.

Jay knew he was screaming, but he couldn't hear his own voice. Nothing could drown out the sound of blood rushing in his ears.

Holding Willi by her neck, the beast pulled her close. He sniffed her, as though she was a piece of meat, a little snack before slipping into the cold dirt to slumber until nightfall. Willi stabbed at the man's shoulder and chest, quick cuts that didn't do any lasting damage. Each thrust of the knife came slower and slower.

The beast was squeezing the life from her.

"*Noooooooo!*"

The vampire turned to face Jay. He held Willi in front of him. She was alive but clearly struggling to keep her eyes open. The Master pushed her shirt aside, exposing the flesh of her neck and shoulder. For the briefest of seconds, Jay imagined the man lowering his mouth to Willi's neck.

Sinking his fangs into her tender flesh.

A heartbeat rumbled in Jay's ears.

It was Willi's.

It had to be.

Weakened as she was, her heart was beating strong, pumping her blood through her body.

Her precious blood.

Master.

Jay shook his head but couldn't get the images out of his mind.

Everything around him slowed down until time seemed to stand still.

The beast ran his tongue down the side of Willi's neck.

Do it.

The beast was toying with him. It knew what Jay had become, and it was demonstrating its control over him.

Fangs bared, ready to plunge into her flesh.

Yes, Master.

Willi's eyes snapped open. She screamed as the beast lowered his mouth to her neck.

Her scream snapped Jay from the beast's hold. He shook his head, clearing the terrible images out of his brain.

"Hey . . . over here. Look at me. C'mon . . . *LOOK AT ME!*" Jay waved his hands at the Master.

The Master looked at Jay.

They locked eyes.

"I'm coming to you," Jay said.

The Master's eyes grew wide in anticipation.

Jay started to run. He turned his focus to Willi and ran faster than he'd ever run in his life. There was no way he could jump over the pit to where they were, so the only thing he could do was run around the perimeter. He had to try to get to her.

To save her.

Jay cut the corner on the other side of the pit. He was only five feet away.

"Willi," he screamed.

Her eyelids were still heavy when she looked at him, but he was sure she could see him.

"*The knife. Toss me the knife,*" Jay screamed.

Willi looked confused, as though she couldn't understand what he was saying.

"*GIVE ME THE KNIFE!*"

Her eyes snapped to attention. She heard him that time.

She lifted her arm and threw the knife. It spun in the air, a slow-motion flash of metal spinning in the darkness. Jay caught the knife as he slid to a halt in front of the beast.

"Let go of her, motherfucker!" he screamed. Jay grabbed the vampire's head, pulling it away from Willi's neck. The beast dropped Willi to deal with this new threat. He grabbed Jay by the shirt. Jay felt himself lifting into the air. The Master tried to fling Jay away, but it was too late.

The knife sunk deep into the beast's neck. Jay quickly pulled it out and stabbed him again.

"The heart," Erick screamed, not dead after all. "*HIT HIM IN THE HEART!*"

Jay brought the knife down to the man's chest with all his might. The blade sliced deep into the beast's flesh, sliding between his ribs. Jay wrenched the knife up, but it wouldn't budge. It was lodged in the beast's ribcage.

The beast quit moving.

Jay let his grip loosen.

Erick came up beside him and rammed the rod into the Master's chest.

Jay backed away. Though he didn't need to breathe, instinct took over, and he could feel his chest heaving. He went to where Willi lay on the ground and inspected her neck, looking for a scratch or a bite mark, anything that would let him know if he'd reacted in time.

Her neck was smooth and unblemished.

Erick used the pole to drag the beast to the pit and held him close to the edge. "Jay, get the knife," he said, "you need to cut off his head."

More than happy to do as he was told, Jay hacked at the beast again and again, cutting deep into his neck. It took some time, but eventually, the man's head detached and fell into the pit. Jay dropped the knife and went back to Willi.

Erick spit on the man and dropped him into the pit.

CHAPTER TWENTY-TWO

WILLI WAS FINE, but a little weak. Jay sat on the ground next to her, hugging her tightly. After a few minutes, she met Jay's eyes. She was crying.

"What's wrong?"

She shook her head. "I can't feel your heartbeat."

Jay knew this already. The beast was dead, but he wasn't back to normal.

Erick was outside the shed, lighting his cloth sacks. When he came back in, he stood over them. "That should work, though it's probably all for nothing. Seriously doubt there's any more of them."

"There must be," Jay said, "he's dead and I'm still a fucking freak."

"Give it a second man. I have to cut out his heart and burn it."

"How are you going to get into the pit?"

Erick looked down into the pit. The drop was at least ten feet. "Hmmm, didn't think about that."

"You didn't think about a lot of shit," said a voice behind them. Fields was sitting up, his lips puffy and bloodied from when Willi punched him.

"Oh, will you please shut the fuck up," Willi said.

"Is Jay back to normal? No. Did dumbass here toss the master into the pit that's too deep to get in and out of? Yes. Yes, he did. Dumbass hunter here didn't think things through."

"Your master's dead," Jay said.

Fields smiled. "Yes, thanks to you, the Master is dead. But this is far from over. My associates are going to want to know what happened here. They're going to ask questions. How do you think they'll react when they find out you killed the Master? I'll tell you. They're going to lose their fucking minds. They're going to get right on to their little planes and fly over here, and then they're going to kill you, and her, and that dumbass over there, and your entire families. They'll set everything up to where it looks like it's all your fault. You're finished, kaput, done . . . dead."

"They aren't going to give a rat's ass what happened here," Erick said. "But you are right about one thing. You're going to catch the blame for all of this."

Fields laughed. "Oh, you think so."

Erick smiled at him. "I know so. Made some phone calls the other day. My people got the ball rolling."

"Bullshit."

They were all quiet for a few minutes. Fields lay on his side, mumbling to himself and giggling intermittently.

Jay could see the sun starting to rise outside the door.

A new day.

Was this it?

Was this all that was left for him? How long could he last like this, before the madness of what he'd become drove him insane, or worse? He looked over at Erick. His weed dealer, a vampire hunter. Who would have thought it? Erick was using a dirty rag to clean the blood and flesh off the prongs of his metal pole. When he'd finished cleaning, he opened his duffle bag and took out a length of rope, which he tossed over to Jay.

"What's this for?" Jay asked, fearing the worst.

"You're going to lower me into the pit so I can get his heart. The rope is in case something happens."

"And then . . . "

"And then what?"

Jay waved his hands in the air. "What about me?"

"Haven't decided yet. I'm thinking once I get his heart

and burn it, maybe that's what it takes . . . right? We're not done here, so that's the only thing I can think of."

"I hope you're right."

"He doesn't know what he's talking about," Willi said.

"You said it, sister," Fields said.

"Shut up," Willi said to Fields.

Erick lay on the fence while Jay hoisted it up. Willi got up and helped push it out above the pit. Jay looked down at the bodies. The beast lay on his back, arms thrown back. His head was over in the corner, staring up at them. Once Erick was positioned directly over the pit, Jay began to lower him down. Stronger than ever, Jay relished his newfound power. There was no way he could have lowered Erick into the pit before he turned. His arms were so strong, the chains felt weightless in his hands. If there was a way scientists could harness all the power without any of the terrible stuff, like the thirst for human blood, vampirism might not be so bad. Jay peered over the edge. "How are you going to get the heart through the fence?"

"I'm not," Erick called back from below, "I'm going to cut it out and hold it through the links while you pull me up."

Once Erick was positioned over the master's body and close enough to reach it through the fence, he pushed the knife through the links and started cutting the man's chest. Though the body was little more than a dusty old corpse now, it still took him a few minutes to crack into the chest cavity. When he had the vampire's heart in his hand, Erick called for Jay to pull him up to the surface. For a second, Jay thought about leaving Erick down there in the pit. Suppose nothing happened when Erick burned the heart? What if Jay didn't return to normal? Jay knew Erick wouldn't waste time taking him down. That was what he did: kill vampires.

He'd told Jay to trust him, but things still weren't right.

"Pull me up."

Jay yanked on the chain, raising his soon-to-be

executioner up from the pit. Willi grabbed the edge of the fence and pulled it away from the pit, and then Jay let up on the chain until the fence rested on the ground. Erick stood, lifted the fence, and picked up the heart. Jay had expected it to be much larger. It was strange to think that this dark and wrinkled thing no bigger than his fist could possibly put an end to this madness.

Erick caught Jay's eye. "Those gas cans in the front room full?"

Jay nodded. "Nothing worse than running out of gas when you're not done mowing."

Fields looked over at Erick. "Planning on burning everything to the ground?"

"You bet your ass."

"Fine with me. Everything's covered under insurance. The remodel is going to be exquisite."

Erick laughed. "You still think you're getting out of this mess? That's fucking hilarious. Guess who's still in handcuffs."

"Not for long."

A shadow now blocked the growing sunlight that had begun illuminating the entrance of the shed.

Everyone turned toward the figure.

A lithe woman with long hair stood in the doorway.

Fields rolled onto his back to get a better look at her. He coughed, and then started giggling. His laughter grew louder and louder.

The woman stepped into the shed. Her gait was slow, more like shuffling than walking. Her head didn't seem to move in time with her body, as though it was wobbling on her neck.

As the woman walked deeper into the shed, her features remained in the shadows, but after a few more stumbling steps, she was close enough for them to see her face.

Jay's mouth went dry.

Fields' laughter and Willi's screams filled the air.

THE SMALL HOURS

LuCyndi shuffled closer to them, her head teetering on her neck as though it was about to fall off. She smiled at them, blood smeared across her fangs. "Hey, everybody," she said, "long time no see."

CHAPTER TWENTY-THREE

LUCYNDI WAS BAREFOOT.
They had buried her with no shoes. That seemed strange to Jay, but he supposed it shouldn't have. When you're dead, you don't need shoes. LuCyndi came closer. Jay could see the dirt caked between her toes. He followed her mud-spattered legs up. She was wearing the white dress Willi had picked out for her funeral. It had a high neckline and looked like something from another era. LuCyndi's mother had insisted on an open casket, and the Puritan neckline was supposed to make it possible. The mortician couldn't fulfill her wishes though, her neck too ravaged by the beast.

That dress.

LuCyndi *was* the lady in white from the park.

She let Frannie go but killed Timothy.

Willi knelt, wheezing. He looked down at her, hoping she wasn't hyperventilating or choking. Her face was twisted in such anguish that it hurt him.

Jay realized he was crying. No tears were coming from his eyes, but he was crying all the same.

LuCyndi touched the ragged holes in her neck where the beast had bitten her. "Figured y'all would be happier to see me," she said.

Willi wailed.

Fields rolled on his side. "Queen, my queen, please . . . please release me from my shackles."

LuCyndi looked down at Fields.

"The handcuffs, my queen. Can you break them for me?"

She knelt next to Fields. "You want me to release you?"

Fields turned his head to look up at her. "Yes . . . yes. Please. You are the Master now."

LuCyndi smiled. She placed her hands under Fields and lifted him up effortlessly, pulling him close. Fields didn't realize what was happening. He laughed gleefully, expecting his new Master to break the cuffs off his wrists.

Instead, she bit down into his neck, cutting off his laughter as his blood flooded her mouth. Fields' feet kicked out, thrashing as she fed on him. It only took a few minutes. Jay couldn't move. He watched, transfixed, unable to break his gaze as she drained the life out of Fields.

His Master.

LuCyndi was the Master now.

Erick stepped up behind him. "She must have fed off the beast. She's his new bride."

"No. No, she can't be his bride," Willi said desperately. "She's my best friend."

"No," Jay said, "Not anymore. She's just like me. We're the same."

Willi looked at Jay, and for the first time, he could see it in her eyes.

She was scared of him.

"Willi, don't . . . everything's going to be okay." Jay reached out to her.

She shrank away from him.

LuCyndi dropped Fields' body on the ground and stood. "I'm the Master," she said, nodding to Jay, "and you're the groom."

Willi looked up at LuCyndi, her eyes wide. "The groom?"

LuCyndi ignored Willi and stepped around her, holding her hand out to Jay. "Come to me."

Jay couldn't stand the sight of her. Rot was already

doing its job, eating away at her skin. He stared at her hand to keep from looking into her eyes. Her fingernails were broken and lined with dirt. She had clawed out of her own coffin, through the six feet of dirt piled on top of her, just to make it back here.

To him.

And though he couldn't look at her dead, slack-jawed face, her empty eyes, he felt that this was it. This was how it all ended for him. She was his Master now. They were destined to be together, forever and ever, forging their own possum kingdom in Grigsby, and maybe even beyond.

The world was theirs for the taking, all they had to do was take it.

He reached for her hand, finally looking up at her face. She was smiling down at him. He looked at her pretty white dress. Sure, it was dirty, but she had come all this way for him. He could see past the dirt.

His bride.

A black stain suddenly appeared and began spreading across LuCyndi's chest. The front of her dress rose from her body, a sharp point threatening to burst through the cloth.

Willi stood behind LuCyndi, pushing Quinten's knife into her back. Jay watched as Willi pulled the knife out and pushed LuCyndi to the ground.

"Fuck you, bitch," Willi screamed, "he's mine."

She stabbed LuCyndi again and again. LuCyndi fought against her, but Willi didn't let up, pushing her down each time she tried to roll away. The blade went in and out, blood flying through the air.

Jay felt weak. Pain erupted in his chest, worse than any pain he'd ever felt in his life. He inhaled deeply, his lungs starved for air.

He could breathe.

He touched his chest, feeling for his pulse.

It was there. Weak, but a pulse.

Willi kept stabbing LuCyndi.

Her eyes were wild.

She screamed as she continued her frenzied attack, and all Jay and Erick could do was watch as she killed her friend. Her friend, who had been killed by a monster and had risen from the grave a monster herself, only to be killed again by her best friend.

Jay no longer felt his pulse.

His vision blurred. Something wasn't right, he was sure of it. "Willi," he said, his voice barely above a whisper. LuCyndi wasn't moving. Erick grabbed Willi's arm, telling her to stop, that she was dead, that it was over.

"Willi." Jay's voice was weak.

They both looked at Jay. "Fuck fuck fuck," Erick said. He scrambled to where Jay now lay on the ground.

Willi looked at the knife in her hand. She was covered in inky blood. "What's wrong?"

"It worked," Erick said, pushing Jay onto his back, "but he's dying."

"What? How?"

Erick straddled Jay and put his hands in the center of his chest. "Going to start CPR. Get your phone ready to call 911."

"911? Are you fucking crazy?"

Erick pumped on Jay's chest. "I told you everything is handled. Don't worry."

"What about all of this?" Willi said, waving her hands at the carnage all around them.

"You think the world is ready for this? Vampires? Better to blame it all on Fields. Official statement . . . Fields held you all at gunpoint and tried to kill you. He was a serial killer, justice is served." He kept pumping Jay's chest. "We cleanse the truth with fire and move the fuck on."

Jay looked over at Willi. She was staring at him, phone in her hand, fingers hovering on the screen. He could feel Erick pounding on his chest, trying to kickstart his heart.

"I'm losing him." Erick did mouth to mouth on Jay, forcing air into his lungs. Jay felt his chest rise with the air, then exhale. He could smell Erick's breath, stale coffee and weed. His vision blurred further. Every single fiber of his body tingled. Deep in the center of his chest, he felt an insistent tug, growing stronger by the second.

Instead of rising to the heavens, Jay was sinking into the ground, unable to resist the undeniable pull of inevitability.

Ashes to ashes.

He was dying, but he was already dead.

Had he been dead for too long?

Dust to dust.

Erick pushed on his chest again. He could feel his ribs cracking with each pump.

You are dust . . .

"Call 911. Tell the dispatcher 'fire in the hole.'"

"Fire in the hole? What does that even mean?"

Erick stopped pumping on Jay's chest. "Trust me. Say 'fire in the hole' and hang up."

And to dust you shall return.

Willi dialed.

Jay began to slip into the ether. It was cold, so cold. The pull of the Earth was strong now. Unbreakable, relentless.

It was cold, but also comforting. Jay felt calm, at peace. Now he could rest.

Yes . . . rest.

Erick was hitting him in the chest.

His body shook from each blow.

Rest . . . rest . . . until the time comes to roam once more . . .

A sickening throb started in his chest. Jay inhaled, air rushing into his lungs. His eyelids fluttered. He didn't want to rest. He took another breath.

He didn't even have to think about it.

"*FIRE IN THE HOLE!*" Willi screamed into the phone.

The pain in his chest expanded, enveloped his entire body.

THE SMALL HOURS

"Hang up the phone," Erick said. He rolled off Jay and lay on the floor next to him, breathing deeply, worn out. Jay couldn't move. The pain radiated out through his whole body.

This was it. The end.

A dull thud rumbled in his chest.

His heartbeat.

The pull of the Earth was weak. He tried to lift his head but couldn't. The harder he fought, the weaker he felt, but the ground was unable to hold him down.

His heart was beating.

Jay took another breath and let it out, coughing.

Willi was right there, leaning over him. "Jay, baby . . . can you hear me?"

Jay smiled weakly at her, nodding. He was back on the surface now.

She grabbed his hand and laid her head on his chest. Jay squeezed Willi's hand tight.

He was never going to let her go.

CHAPTER TWENTY-FOUR

ERICK DIDN'T HAVE to burn Fields' house down after all. Within minutes, a team of three agents wearing hazmat suits arrived and began cleanup. Erick led Jay and Willi out of the shed and back into the Fields' house. Jay slumped on the sofa to get his strength back while Willi and Erick went through the kitchen and living room wiping down everything they could have come into contact with.

"What about this?" Willi asked, pointing at Arty and the coagulated pool of blood by the recliner.

"They'll get it. Don't worry, they've been doing this shit for years. In a few days, someone from the FBI will be here."

"The FBI?"

"Don't worry, they work with me. It'll just be a debriefing. In the meantime, you know nothing. Do. Not. Talk. To. Anyone. Got it?"

Willi and Jay nodded.

"What's the official story?" Jay asked.

"It was Fields, all of it. Blame him for everything. It'll hit the news hard, might go national, but the good thing about living in America is it's only a matter of time before another crazy news story comes around to make everyone forget about one more serial killer."

When they walked out of Fields' house, the team that had been working in the shed was gone, as were the cars from the driveway. The sun was shining but there was a slight chill in the air. They stood on Fields' back porch away from prying eyes.

"How did they . . . " Willi asked, waving at the empty driveway.

"They're professionals. They'll bring Fields' car back tonight, then they'll torch the shed. There's no way they'll be able to keep that a secret, so expect the local fire department on site. Don't say anything and everything will be fine. You were right about Fields, he was Russian mob. He didn't even own his house. A private group holds the deed, and I imagine they'll release it back to a realtor and it'll go on the market."

"What if they install another operative?" Jay asked.

"Not likely. Just think, in a month or two, you'll have a new neighbor."

"Hopefully one that doesn't have a pet vampire," Willi said.

Erick held out his hand. "Glad you made it back," he said to Jay.

Jay shook his hand. "Would you have . . . if things . . . "

Erick smiled grimly. "In a heartbeat. But I didn't have to."

"You sticking around?" Willi asked.

Erick nodded. "Yeah, I'll be around. Too many customers needing a good smoke."

Jay shook his head. "Not me, I'm done." He looked down at his feet for a second, and then back up at them. "Time to get my shit together." He looked at Willi. "I'm serious."

She smiled at him.

"Dying will do that to you," Erick said, "but if you ever need anything, you know where to find me."

Back at Jay's house, Willi and Jay went into his bedroom and stared at themselves in his mirror. They were both filthy, with blood, gore, and mud smeared on their faces and hair.

"These clothes are going to have to be burned," Jay said.

Willi sat on his bed. Jay sat next to her, unable to hold

it in anymore. He looked at her with tears in his eyes. "I fucked up so bad."

"Why are you saying that?"

"Quinten? Arty? You realize we have more funerals in our future now, right?"

"Baby, there will always be funerals in our future. The best we can hope for is for time to do its job and keep the last one a distant memory. Without you putting everything together like you did, LuCyndi wouldn't have justice."

Jay nodded. "I love you."

Willi leaned in close and kissed Jay. "I love you too," she said. Jay hugged her tight as they fell back on the bed, hoping to keep holding the embrace forever.

"What kind of job are you looking to get?" Willi asked.

Jay rolled on his back and stared at the ceiling. "You know, I'm kinda thinking about going into the vampire hunting business."

Willi sat up and stared at Jay, her eyes wide. "Are you fucking crazy?"

ACKNOWLEDGMENTS

They say books are never written alone. Except in this case, it was. Absolutely no A.I. was used in the inception, creation, and execution of this book. I must thank Max Booth III, for not just being the publisher of this book, but for encouraging me to write it in the first place. After I pitched them the initial idea, they said I HAD to write the story. The idea: What if the Russians caught Dracula on the *Demeter* when he was escaping Europe? What if it happened now, in Texas? Knowing full well they could have completely rejected the finished project, I am eternally grateful Max took a chance with this book to put it out into the world. I would also like to thank Michael David Wilson, my podcast co-host, but more importantly, one of the best friends anyone could have. He's always been on my side, always full of encouragement and inspiration. I would also like to thank early beta readers Brennan LaFaro, Mackenzie Kiera, and Thomas Joyce for taking the time to read the first draft of this book when it was still struggling to find its footing. Lastly, thanks to Tom Holland, Christopher Walken, and Bram Stoker. Stoker's inclusion is obvious, and if you've paid attention, you know why I would thank Tom Holland. Christopher Walken . . . well, without him masterfully stealing every scene in *Suicide Kings*, this book might not have ever seen the light of day, so thank you!

ABOUT THE AUTHOR

Bob Pastorella is the co-host of the This Is Horror podcast. He is also the author of *They're Watching* (with Michael David Wilson), with numerous tales in such publications as *Lost Films, Borderlands 6, Warmed & Bound: a Velvet Anthology*, and the *Booked Anthology*. *The Small Hours* is Bob's debut solo novel. Bob lives in southeast Texas with his cat, Squeaky, and is currently working on another vampire story.

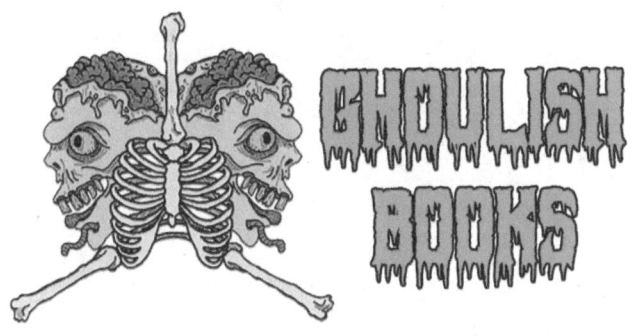

Patreon:
www.patreon.com/ghoulishbooks

Website:
www.Ghoulish.rip

Facebook:
www.facebook.com/GhoulishBooks

Bluesky:
@ghoulish.bsky.social

Instagram:
@GhoulishBookstore

Linktree:
linktr.ee/ghoulishbooks